CARL L

KNOWING THINGS

carlleeuk.com
facebook.com/carlleeuk

Cover Art by BeePea Design.

Dedicated to
Glyn.
A wit and a gentleman.

PROLOGUE

The old man sat in the chair, his arthritic fingers stroking the white beard flowing from his jaw. His eyes no longer burned with the same ferocity, though they occasionally flickered with the memory of it. He no longer moved with the urgency of youth, though his purpose remained. Sort of.

"None of us are getting any younger," said Jobe, looking over at the old boss from across the room.

"I'm just saying, maybe he's not as focused as he used to be," argued Aran, his colleague, sat at the terminal next to him.

"Seems alright to me," said Jobe, now turning back to his friend.

"He pissed himself this morning... just sat there, didn't even notice... literally sat there with piss dripping off his chair."

"And you've never pissed yourself?"

"Not since I was ten," said Aran, gobsmacked. "Have you?"

"No," he said a little too quickly. "I just… I just meant… look, so he's got a weak bladder. He's old. It doesn't mean that he doesn't still have his wits about him."

"The other day, he forgot to get dressed. Just strolled in, wearing nothing but his boots, eating a slice of burnt toast."

"He always eats burnt toast."

"I think you're missing the point," said Aran. "I'm simply saying that maybe he's not quite as 'on it' as he used to be. I always used to understand the decisions that got made in here, but lately… lately, I'm struggling to understand a lot of the thinking that's going on."

"He's always known what he's doing," Jobe argued, "and he's never exactly been one to argue with."

"He always 'used to' know what he was doing…"

"Well, maybe it's a phase?" Jobe suggested.

"Yeah, a phase of aging… that being one of the later stages, just before you get to the last phase and stop aging altogether. I mean, how old is he, anyway?"

"Nobody knows. He refuses to be defined by years."

"It doesn't even matter," Aran put his hands up. "When you start pissing yourself and walking around with your tackle out, you're maybe getting a little bit too long in the tooth for the big job."

"I think you're forgetting that he created the big job. It's his company. Nobody would even begin to know how to do what he does… unless you're putting yourself up for the role?"

"That would be a big 'no' from me."

"Then, who?" Jobe asked, looking around the room at the twenty or more colleagues sat at their terminals. "Cindy?"

"Cindy?" Aran repeated, with something bordering on horror. "Mud has more common sense than Cindy. I once saw her try

5

to eat soup with a fork."

"What about... Jerry?"

"Now you're just being silly. We both know that Jerry shouldn't really be allowed in the same room as other people. The man bored his own mother to death..."

"I'm pretty sure that didn't actually happen," Jobe interrupted.

"It did," Aran insisted. "Ted told me."

"Alright. What about Ted?"

"No. Not Ted. You can't trust a word he says. The man talks out of his arse."

"I rest my case," Aran said. "There is nobody to replace him."

"That is not a good thing," said Jobe, as the old man leaned into a microphone next to his chair.

"Today, I would like you all to call me Captain Artichoke and there's a pack of broken biscuits in it for anyone who has seen my boat."

BEFORE THE KNOWING

ONE

CHAPEL-ON-THE-MOSS, MIDDLESWORTH

"It's never been my intention to go into law," said Blake, as he strolled along the side of the river, talking into his phone. "I'm not even studying anything remotely linked with law!"

The sun hadn't quite managed to peek from behind the clouds, though it was trying and so there was still a bit of a chill to the morning and the scent of the honeysuckle from the hedgerows went with his every step.

"I don't know where he got the idea," Blake continued. "Maybe he dreamt it, but he definitely didn't get it from me."

It was his favourite walk, along the side of the river, not that he was paying much attention to it, side-tracked as he was with would-be career talk. Usually, the beauty of the riverside, the colour palette of the hedgerows, the smells and the tranquillity of the walk down to the old chapel itself was a therapy to the pressures of university and its endless lectures, not that he attended many of them.

He wasn't much of a bookworm. It never ceased to amaze him that he had ended up at university at all. He had more or less coasted along without really thinking about anything he was doing. He had picked his courses with little conviction, more to be seen to be doing something than targeting any potential future career. It wasn't that he was unintelligent, he was as clever as the next person, but he didn't have a strong inclination as to what he wanted to do and so had figured it was better to be doing something than nothing at all, no matter how half-arsed he did it.

He wasn't a social butterfly either. He enjoyed a spliff every now and then with Mason, a stoner he had known since high school, and occasionally went for a beer or a coffee with Olivia, a girl he had known since junior school. That was more-or-less the bulk sum of his social interactions and that was just fine by him. He found the vast majority of people to be a combination of irritating, self-absorbed, obnoxious, greedy and outright ridiculous.

"I'll talk to you later, Mum," he said, before placing the phone in his jacket pocket. It was a new black, three-quarter length jacket, wool and cashmere and though he wasn't normally particular when it came to brands or clothing styles in general, he couldn't help but feel good about himself when he wore it and had even brushed his unruly blaze of reddish-brown hair before leaving the house.

The river veered right and the path gave way to a rough track through a small wooded area, around six feet away from the river itself. Shafts of sunlight had started to dance through the trees as the breeze brushed the branches, causing the dirt track to light up sporadically, like some sort of natural disco floor. Blake started humming a Bee Gees song as he went.

This part of the river was always quiet, host to the occasional dog walker. It was also the best short-cut to Olivia's house on the other side of the chapel.

After being momentarily distracted by a white butterfly fluttering by his face, he spotted a man standing in the river.

A naked man, perhaps in his late forties, cropped hair, standing absolutely still, almost up to his waist in the middle of the river.

Blake continued walking, slower now, his interest peaked. As he approached, the man seemed to ignore him, keeping his gaze firmly on the water, as if entranced.

Blake resisted the urge to reach for his phone in order to take a snap for social media. Just.

"Hello?" he ventured, tentatively, not wanting to alarm the man. "Are you alright?"

The man kept his focus, if indeed that was what it was, his eyes never leaving the water.

Blake looked around to see if there was anyone else that might be able to offer assistance, but it was a secluded spot and he knew full well that a second opinion on the matter was unlikely to come along any time soon.

"Would you like some help?" he asked.

The man looked up at him, his eyes wide and worried and he put his finger to his lips. "Shh. They're listening."

"Okay," said Blake, looking around again, scanning for anyone to whom the man might be referring. "Who's listening, the fish?" he asked.

The man shot him an annoyed glance. "Don't be so bloody stupid!"

"I'm sorry," Blake said, defensively. "It was just that you were... well, you were just staring into the water. I... I didn't know..."

"Shh," the man repeated.

Blake looked around again, flummoxed. Was he part of some kind of practical joke? He couldn't see anyone with a camera.

"Listen, I'm going to call an ambulance."

"No," the man snapped. "No ambulance. I'm fine."

"I think that might be debatable," Blake replied.

"Leave me alone," the man added. "I'm fine."

"It's just that I think you actually might not be fine. I mean, where are your clothes?" he asked, scanning the riverbank for a discarded bundle.

"I got rid of them. I can't find the tracker."

"What tracker?" he asked, unsure as to whether he wanted to know the answer or not.

"Shh! Just leave me alone. Trust me. I know what I'm doing."

"With respect, you don't look like someone who knows what they're doing."

The man gave out a huge sigh. "You wouldn't understand."

"I imagine not, but a doctor might."

"No ambulance!" he snapped again. "Why can't you just be like everybody else and mind your own business?"

"I'm just trying to be helpful, that's all."

"Well, it would be helpful to me if you just minded your own business."

Blake took the phone out of his pocket.

"Please, don't do that," said the man. "If you make that call, I'm as good as dead."

He began to shiver as he stood there looking back at Blake

from the water, with sincere eyes.

"Okay," Blake said, though no more words came quickly to mind. "I'll be honest, I'm a bit unsure as to what to do next in this situation."

"I get that," said the man. "I completely understand that from where you're standing, it might look like I'm having a bit of a meltdown."

"I'm really glad you said that, because you were sort of acting like you weren't."

"I'm *not* having a meltdown," the man thought for a moment. "Well, I suppose I am. It's complicated."

Blake nodded. He imagined it *was* complicated. He imagined there was a very long and winding explanation for why the man had stripped naked and wandered into the middle of a river to stare at water.

"Where did you put your clothes?" Blake asked.

"I took them off in the water, so…" his gaze floated down river, following the course his clothes had taken.

"Right, only I think we need to get you out of the water."

"Not until I find the tracker," the man shook his head and started rubbing a hand over his neck and shoulders.

"I don't understand," said Blake.

"You don't need to understand. Listen, there must be a chip in me and it doesn't work so well in or around water. That's why I got in here. I need to find it and get rid of it."

"This is going to sound like kind of an obvious question…" Blake began, "but why do you have a chip in you?"

"You don't need to know," he said, continuing to grope himself. "You don't happen to have a metal detector, do you?"

"No, but I know a man who does," Blake replied, without thinking.

"Really?" the man asked, momentarily pausing his self-massage session.

"Well, yeah," he replied, silently cursing himself for opening his mouth.

"Do you think you could borrow it?"

"Erm, I'm not really sure," he said, trying his best to back-track.

"Could you ask?"

Blake looked at his phone and sighed.

TWO

Olivia made her way to the allotment, wearing some jeans and a cream top that she had thrown on in a hurry. She had also put her long, blonde hair in a ponytail to save time. Blake hadn't been specific at all, which had both intrigued and frustrated her, but he had asked her to bring some clothes to fit a medium-sized man (her dad's clothes loosely fit the bill) and to go and see The Onion Sage at the allotment.

The Onion Sage wasn't his real name, obviously. It was a name that Olivia had coined some years back, due to the fact the he grew onions (amongst other things) and had a lot of stories to tell. He was actually called Arthur.

Arthur was a sweet old man who was almost always at the allotment, it was his entire world. As kids, Olivia and Blake had played out down by the allotments, there were a couple of good jumps down that way for the bikes. Arthur had once repaired a puncture on Blake's bike and they had known him ever since.

He was as pleasant as they came, but had the habit of talking in riddles a great deal of the time. Olivia was sure that the man was under the impression that he was imparting some great wisdom when he spoke. The truth was that it rarely made much sense. They humoured him, of course. He was harmless and they found him quite amusing to be honest. Occasionally, especially in recent years, Blake had tried to correct the man, but he always continued undeterred, as if oblivious.

She didn't know his age. Maybe Blake did, but he had never said. She surmised he must have been in his late eighties by now and looked every inch of it, from his bobble-hat to his wellies and the old brown corduroys and blue shirt in between.

She walked up to the allotment and opened the rickety old wooden gate, before making her way over to his shed.

It wasn't a huge area, home to just a dozen plots in a long thin line, nestled behind the local park grounds. Arthur's plot was at the top of the allotment and she could see him slumped in his deck chair, outside his shed.

"Morning, Arthur!" she called to him.

"Morning, Liv!" he waved back, his thick Cornish twang jolly, as ever. "Not seen you in a while," he added.

"University!"

"Blake not with you?"

"Not at the minute, although he's the one that asked me to stop by."

He sat forward in the deck chair.

She reached his plot and put her backpack down on the ground for a moment. "Planted anything new today?"

"Beetroot. The thinking man's vegetable."

"Right." She didn't ask why. "Can you remember that old metal detector you used to have a few years ago?"

"The Scarlet Raven?"

"Um, yeah? If that was… what it was called?"

"Still got her in the shed!" he said, as if the very memory of it brought him some joy.

"Excellent…"

"She still goes like a dream, you know? Did I ever tell you about the stash of Roman coins she found down on the wild field on Potter's Hill?"

"Once or twice," she nodded. "Would I be able to borrow it?"

"I don't see any reason why not." He stood from the deck chair and went into the shed. It was only a small structure, in truth only the cobwebs keeping it up, but it seemed to have absolutely everything in it, including a decidedly unsafe light bulb, wired to the mains supply, using mainly a blend of guesswork and hope. Still, it occasionally worked and hadn't set fire to anything yet.

He moved one or two items out of the way before reaching towards the back and pulling out the old metal detector.

"I'll bring it straight back. Shouldn't be much more than an hour or so."

"No problem," he said, handing it over. "She's hungry, this one. Keep her low and let her go."

"Right," Olivia nodded politely.

"Seek and ye shall find," he added.

"That's great, thanks." She picked up her backpack and set off for the river. "I'll be back soon!"

Arthur returned to his deck chair, slumping down to rest and survey his plot, keeping a watchful eye on his beetroot.

THREE

"This was not what I expected," she said, handing the metal detector over to Blake.

"I'm having difficulty getting my head round it too," he said.

"Why is he naked?"

"Something to do with a chip," he replied, though there was little in the way of conviction to his delivery.

Blake checked the detector, reminding himself of the controls. He had used it once before, though it was some years ago and he hadn't been entirely sure of them the last time round.

"Right, you'll need to get out of the water," Blake said.

"There's a towel and some clothes and shoes in the bag," Olivia said, putting the backpack down by Blake's feet. She then turned around to give the man an ounce of privacy as he waded against the steady flow of the river and scrambled up

17

the banking.

Blake grabbed the towel from the bag and cautiously handed it to him as he stood trembling. He still wasn't convinced that the man was a full deck.

The man patted himself dry and then quickly put on a pair of boxer shorts from the bag, before draping the towel over his shoulders.

"Is it on?" he asked, referring to the detector.

Blake flicked the switch. "It is now."

"Okay, scan it all over me," he said, slowly moving around as Blake held the detector just a few inches away from his skin. After a few sporadic noises as it started up, Blake manoeuvred the device over the man's body, shoulders first and then chest, privates and legs.

"Right, turn around," Blake said, humouring the man.

He did so and Blake moved the device from the back of his head, down his back, until it beeped at his backside.

"Oh," Blake said. He obviously hadn't expected there to be any truth to the man's ramblings. "That's your arse."

"That makes sense," the man mumbled to himself.

"Does it?" Blake asked.

"Somebody put a chip up your arse?" Olivia said, confusion belying her blank expression.

"You're on your own getting that out," said Blake.

"Not *up* my arse," the man replied, feeling his buttocks through the shorts. "It's in the cheek. Lot of meat to protect and hide it… there it is!"

"I'm struggling to understand what's going on," Olivia said.

"Have either of you got a knife?" asked the man.

"No. And I don't think it's the best idea to let you have a knife," said Blake.

18

"Just stop!" Olivia said, firmly. "This is ridiculous!"

The man looked at her, Blake too, both a little taken back at her forcefulness and looking more than a little like reprimanded children.

"What's your name?" she asked the man.

"You don't need to know and you're better off not knowing," he replied.

"You'll give me your name or I'm calling the police, because this is just... weird!"

He looked around, as if to make sure the coast was clear and then sheepishly offered his name. "Ven."

"Right, thank you. Now, Ven, what the hell is going on with you?"

"Look. I can't tell you. Not everything, because you wouldn't believe it anyway and I don't have the time to explain, but what I can tell you is that I have a chip in my arse cheek that needs taking out. That needs to happen really quickly or I'm going to be in a heap of trouble. Now, I thank you for the clothes and the lend of the metal detector, I really do, but right now I need a knife."

The man seemed to have recovered to some degree from whatever had caused him to freeze up in the water and now sounded sincere and urgent.

"I don't have a knife, but I know a man who will have," said Blake. "Get dressed. It's not far."

FOUR

"He's got a chip in his arse?" Arthur repeated back to them.

"Yeah," Blake replied. "That's what we needed the metal detector for."

"Why'd you put a chip in your arse?" Arthur asked the man directly now.

"*I* didn't."

"Right, so you've been chipped then?" he asked, a puzzled look resting between the lines on his face.

"Yes," he nodded. "And I urgently need it taking out."

"You know I'm not a surgeon, right?"

"Trust me, I am very much aware of that," Ven replied, looking the man up and down, as a white plastic bag blew off the back of the shed door and across the allotment. "I wouldn't be asking if it wasn't urgent."

Arthur looked at the man, long and hard, eyeing up the ill-fitting suit trousers and shirt.

"Alright," he decided. "A man in need is a potential good deed."

"Okay," said Ven, his eyes flitting from the old man to Blake and Olivia.

"He does that," Blake said, quietly, as Arthur wandered into his shed. "It's a 'wisdom' thing, the rhyming."

"Right," Ven said, nervously looking around the allotment and the surrounding trees, willing the old man to hurry up.

Blake noted the man's anxiety. He had seemed very nervy on the walk to the allotment and that combined with the whole 'chip in the arse' situation had Blake more than a little confused and perhaps mildly anxious himself.

"Right then," announced Arthur, returning from his shed with a Stanley knife and pair of pliers. "There's a stool in the shed. Drop your trousers and bend over it and let's have a look."

Olivia thought she heard the man gulp down his fear, before heading for the shed and baring his arse to The Onion Sage.

Ven ran a finger over his right buttock until he thought he could feel the slight lump that the metal detector had found.

"There," he said, pointing to the spot.

"Okay," said Arthur, sticking the knife into his cheek.

"Argh! Jesus!" Ven yelped.

"What?"

"You might have at least given me a countdown!"

"Do it quick, just the trick," came the reply.

Ven gritted his teeth as he felt the knife moving within the cheek.

Blake and Olivia stood still, watching from outside the shed.

"This is not how I thought my day would turn out," she said, watching the blood dribble down the man's thigh.

"Got it!" Arthur declared after another moment's rummaging. He pulled the chip free with the pliers to reveal something resembling a black three-amp fuse, but half the size.

"Thank God!" Ven exclaimed. "Let me see."

Arthur handed it over to the man before reaching for a hip flask and pouring a lick of brandy on to the wound.

"Argh! Jesus!" Ven yelped again. "Warn me!"

"I got a plaster in here somewhere, bear with me," he replied, oblivious to the man's protests.

"Why would somebody put a chip in your arse?" Blake asked again, hoping that the man might be more inclined to answer now.

Arthur slapped a plaster over the small cut. "There. You're good to pull your trousers up."

The man did so, straightening up and leaving the shed, holding the chip up in front of his eyes and scrutinising it. He then dropped it on to the paving slab in front of him and stamped down hard, crushing the chip into the concrete.

"You're really not going to give us an answer, after all that?" Blake pushed.

"Listen," the man started, "I really can't thank you enough for what you've done... this..." he motioned to the shed, "the clothes. Please believe me when I say that you are much better off not knowing why someone put a chip in my arse, but know that what you've done has probably saved my life."

The man seemed sincere and genuinely apologetic at the lack of information he could give. Blake still wanted to know, but felt at least appreciated for the assistance he had given and it looked like that would have to be enough.

The man started walking away from them and out of the allotment, pausing at the decrepit gate to look back and thank them all once again.

And then he was gone.

Blake looked at Olivia, shaking his head in bewilderment and then turned to Arthur, who had plonked himself back down into his deck chair.

"Strange sort, wasn't he?" Arthur said, reflectively.

"Just a bit," Olivia agreed.

"Yeah, sorry about that, Arthur," said Blake. "I know it was a weird thing to ask, but you were the first person I thought of and the nearest too."

"No bother," Arthur said, pulling a carrot from out of the soil by the side of the deck chair and taking a bite.

"Are you not supposed to wash those first?" Blake asked.

"A bit of dirt doesn't hurt."

"A bit? It's completely covered in it!"

"Yeah, but it's my dirt," Arthur eventually said after chewing in contemplation for a moment.

FIVE

Irene's Kettle was the only café in Chapel-on-the-Moss and like the village itself, it was quiet. There was the occasional rambler around lunchtime, a few retired folk here and there, resting their legs from walking the dog, but aside from that it was usually empty. Just the way Blake liked it.

Irene herself was fast approaching something like five-hundred years old, Blake assumed. She had a permanent look of bewilderment on her face, especially when taking an order and moved with the speed of a tortoise pulling a tractor.

She emerged from the kitchen, tray in hand with two mugs shaking across it and very slowly started to make her way over to them at their seat by the window. Blake stood to take the tray from her.

"Thanks, Irene," he said, taking the weight of the tray and then placing it on the table.

"You're welcome, dear," she replied in a fragile voice, before turning and shuffling back into the kitchen.

"Still going strong," Olivia smiled.

"Well, she's still going. I don't know about strong."

"Give over," she chastised him, playfully, as they both took a sip of their drink.

"Tea, yeah?" he asked.

She nodded. "You ordered coffees though?"

He nodded. "Yep. Could be worse. At least she boiled the kettle this time."

It was a tiny café, situated just off the main street (although main street seemed like such a grand title for the row of a dozen or so weathered-stone houses, one of which was a corner shop that sold newspapers and very little else and another that often had a collapsible table out front with homemade cakes on and an honesty box). The small counter took up a third of the café, leaving just enough room for three aging tables and an assortment of chairs and stools from across the ages.

Though it was hardly troubling the big chains in the nearby town, a few miles south, it reflected the charm of the village and clearly gave Irene something else to do besides whistling off-key to whatever garbage was on the radio in the kitchen.

"What a morning!" Olivia said.

"I know. Thanks for getting the clothes, by the way."

"No worries."

"Was your dad okay with you taking them?"

"Oh, I didn't *ask* him," she laughed. "He hasn't even got a clue what clothes he's got! He wears the same stuff all the time. I'd be surprised if he realises anything's gone."

"Fair enough. Thanks anyway."

25

"What do you think it was all about?" she asked, following the question with a sip of tea.

"I haven't got a clue. It's been the weirdest morning since that tramp set his shoes on fire at the bus stop."

"I remember that," she chuckled at the memory. "Old Harold had to talk him down from off the roof of the bus shelter."

"Enticed him down with a can of cider, if I recall."

"Yeah. I think today was weirder though," she concluded. "I mean, I put it down to some sort of mid-life crisis… maybe seen one too many spy thrillers perhaps…"

"Me too" he agreed, "until we found the chip."

They both returned to their respective brews, taking a drink and allowing the morning's events to replay and ruminate.

"I think it keeps boiling down to the same question. Why would someone put a chip in his arse?" he finally said.

"Didn't he say it was a tracking chip?"

"Yeah. So someone wanted to keep tabs on him and he definitely seemed scared about what would happen if he didn't remove it."

"MI5?" she guessed.

"Could be," he agreed. "Some sort of government thing, it has to be."

"My Uncle Gary used to think he was being followed by government officials," she said.

"Really?" Blake was surprised. "And was he?"

"Store detectives," she replied. "He was a bit of a kleptomaniac. Loved his conspiracy theories though. He always used to say that they put things in margarine to make you more susceptible to mind control."

"Wow."

"Yeah. He would only ever eat butter."

"Well, butter is actually the better option…" Blake began.

"He also refused to believe that there was such a thing as the solar system," she interrupted.

"Oh."

"He said that the whole 'space thing' was an elaborate lie to extort money, under the guise of scientific grants given to numerous departments and corporations for other nefarious purposes."

"Was your Uncle Gary on drugs?"

"Yeah," she confirmed. "Almost all of them, I think."

"At least the day can't get any weirder. What have you got planned for the afternoon?"

"I'm writing an essay on the importance of cheese throughout the ages."

Blake sniggered and then realised she wasn't joking. "Oh."

"It's actually part of a larger study about the impact of different foods throughout history," she explained.

"Oh," he repeated.

"It's not as interesting as it sounds," she smiled.

"It doesn't sound interesting at all."

"And what magnificent thing are you up to?" she asked.

"I plan to spend the afternoon avoiding essays completely. I've got some serious high-level lounging to do."

"Call Of Duty?" she guessed.

"Probably."

"Well, unlike you, I actually want some grades by the end of university life," she laughed. "Have you even thought about what you're going to do after uni?"

"I've thought about it, yeah," he replied, somewhat flippantly.

"Call Of Duty?"

"Probably."

"Cataracts have more focus than you," she said, shaking her head.

"I just haven't found anything that excites me yet, certainly nothing that makes me want to commit my life to it. What if I pick the wrong thing?"

"You can always unpick it, you know," she said, casting an eye through the window to the street beyond. "Try something and if you don't like it, move along and try something else."

"I suppose so. What are your long-term career plans then?" he asked, but her attention was glued on her view from the window. "Hello?"

"Huh?" she said, still not looking his way.

"Am I boring you?"

"Sorry. There was a guy on the corner of Main Street... just looked a bit odd."

"How do you mean?"

"Just awkward. Tall, smart-looking, black jacket..."

"Doesn't sound that odd," Blake said, gulping down half a mug of tea. "If you'd have said space suit..."

"It was just the way he was acting. He had something in his hand... moving around with it, like he was scanning something."

"Probably his phone... might have been on Google Maps or something."

"Maybe."

"I think this morning has got you spooked," he chuckled. "Either that or all that writing about cheese has started to addle your mind," he added, standing.

"You're probably right," she said, also standing and grabbing her bag from by the side of her seat. "What are you up to tonight? Going up to The Griffin?" she asked, referring to the student bar in the neighbouring town.

"No, I'll leave it tonight. Maybe tomorrow? I'll give you a call."

"Well, enjoy your twenty hours of Call Of Duty," she said, heading for the door.

"Thanks, Irene!" they both shouted before leaving the café. She didn't hear them, as usual.

SIX

His afternoon lounging had culminated in a three-hour nap, because doing nothing could be extremely tiring. This had led to a later-than-normal evening meal of toast, followed by half a pack of shortbread biscuits. His parents had long since given up on asking him to join them for dinner, opting to leave him to his own devices, those being largely quick and unhealthy.

He washed another biscuit down with a glass of milk as his phone rang, the caller ID showing as his friend.

"Hi, Mason. What's up?" he asked.

"Not much. Just got some new green in," replied the stoner.

"That's good," Blake said, with little interest. He didn't mind the odd drag here and there, but in truth, it didn't hold much in the way of fascination for him.

Mason, on the other hand, was consumed by weed. It was as if it was his sole purpose in life, to discover each and every strain of the stuff and smoke it, in every conceivable way and log each individual high. Every conversation Blake had ever had with the guy had somehow come back to weed.

In many ways, Blake envied the passion and commitment his friend had for the stuff. At least he knew what he wanted to do with his life. It wasn't much, if anything really, but he was determined to see it through, regardless.

Blake just couldn't summon the drive for anything. Not yet at least. He hoped that perhaps inspiration was just around the corner, waiting to pounce and get him hooked.

His dad was always talking about law, probably because he was a lawyer, but Blake hated the thought of going down that route. It sounded like a good deal of hard, boring work to finally get to the point where you were qualified to do a good deal more hard, boring work, until you eventually retired. Yes, it was good money, but there had to more to life than just that!

And that was the cut of it. He just couldn't imagine doing one thing for the rest of his life, regardless of what that one thing was. Not when there were so many things to choose from and he hadn't even scratched the surface looking at exactly what those options were.

One career. One wife. One house in one town… how did people do it? *Not that he wanted numerous wives*, but how did people choose and how was one of anything enough for anyone?

"What are you up to, man?" Mason asked.

"Just finishing my tea," Blake replied, staring at the remaining half pack of biscuits on his bed.

"It's after nine o'clock," Mason said. "You've not had anything with cheese in, have you? That shit will mess with

31

your mind if you eat it too late on."

Blake almost laughed at the comment. How would cheese mess with his mind any more than the weed was messing with Mason's?

"No cheese. Shortbread biscuits."

"Ah, man!" Mason exclaimed, his mouth watering at the thought. "I need to get me some of those."

"I need to stop eating them. I've already eaten half the pack."

There was a pause on the other end of the line for a moment. "Mason?"

"Sorry, man," he replied. "I'm just looking out of my window and there's some blue flashing lights over in the woods."

"Is it the police?" Blake asked.

"Nah, man. These are all over the place, not like on a car."

"Oh," Blake said, trying to think hard on what his friend could be seeing.

"Probably fae folk, man."

"Fae folk?"

"Yeah," Mason continued. "I was reading somewhere about how fairies and pixies really come alive at night, when nobody's watching."

Blake shoved a whole biscuit into his mouth and started chewing. "But *you're* watching," he said, spitting crumbs over his t-shirt.

"Yeah, but they don't know I'm watching."

"Okay. You been smoking a lot tonight?" Blake asked.

"Yeah, man," Mason chuckled. "I'm baked."

"Thought so," Blake said, before deciding to not only humour his friend, but actually encourage him. "Could be UFOs," he added.

"It could be UFOs!" he parroted back. "Man, the government always try and cover that shit up!"

"I'll catch you later!" Blake smiled and ended the call, safe in the knowledge that his friend was about to spend the rest of the night knee-deep in conspiracy theories.

SEVEN

It was almost 1am.

Detective Marv Weaving had resorted to slapping himself around the face to stay awake. It was a tactic his younger partner, Connor Raines couldn't get used to.

"You do know there's coffee in the flask?" Connor said. "You don't have to resort to sadistic rituals."

Marv reached into the footwell for the flask.

They were parked outside one of the terraced cottages lining the road, between two other parked cars and they were a fair distance away from the churchyard that they were keeping an eye on.

The good people of Chapel-on-the-Moss had been perturbed of late. The news that several of the carved stone grotesques in the churchyard had been stolen had unsettled the residents to a degree and the two investigators had been ordered to post watch over the place in an effort to determine the culprits.

Of course Marv had sighed when handed the case. Surely just bored kids with nothing better to do. He was more than a little cynical these days, fast approaching as he was, a full decade in the job.

And what a dream job it had seemed back in his mid-twenties, a chance to work on the Middlesworth Investigations Team, to help solve the countless cases and to pit his wits against the deadliest and most cunning criminals.

Of course, it hadn't quite played out like that. In truth, Marv had become quite bored and disenchanted with the role of 'monitoring nut jobs' and pointing out the blatantly obvious to the 'slow and easily bewildered'. Couple that with the feeling of disappointment at having nothing even remotely interesting to do most of the time and it was enough to muster a good deal of professional resentment.

Connor was in his late twenties, however, and hadn't been working for the team even half as long as Marv and perhaps it was for that reason alone that he still maintained a modicum of enthusiasm for his work.

"Three nights now," Marv moaned as he poured himself some coffee from the flask into a plastic cup. "Three nights of staring at this street, drinking what can only be described as warm sludge."

"I thought you would be glad to be out of the house," Connor smiled, referring to the often chaotic home life that his partner usually endured.

"I don't mind being in the house at this time, she's asleep. It's when she's awake that I have the problem. You know what she said to me the other day?" Marv asked.

35

"I have no idea," Connor answered, though he guessed he was about to find out.

"She wants to start a family!"

"What, with you?" Connor smiled now.

"Exactly! That's what I said!" Marv exclaimed. "Honestly, sometimes it's like she's never even met me. In the four years we've worked together, have I ever struck you as a person who wants to start a family?"

"You've barely even struck me as a person," Connor replied. "Although, a few kids might be just the thing."

Marv stared at his colleague. "Just the thing for what... violent suicide? I can't imagine anything worse than waking up to discover a whining little snot machine screaming in my face. It's bad enough having to wake up next to *that* grumpy twat."

"You know, she probably says the same about you. You're not exactly the cheeriest man in the world."

Marv shrugged his shoulders and took a drink from the steaming cup of coffee. It was a pleasant summer's night, so the coffee was more about staying awake than keeping warm.

"I really would have thought they would have taken another statue by now. I thought it was one every other night?" Connor asked.

"It was."

Connor flicked at his cheek as he thought, the popping sound it produced clearly not impressing his partner.

"Sorry, is that annoying?" he asked.

Marv looked at his partner. "No, it's the best thing ever," he said, sarcasm drenching the sentence.

"Did we even check to see if there were any more statues to take?" Connor said. "I mean, how many are in there?"

"A dozen originally, I think. Nine more to go."

They both stared back out to the churchyard, the moonlight clipping some of the gravestones and creating a typical horror movie scene.

"Did you ever see the third Exorcist movie?" Connor asked.

"Nope," Marv replied, without interest.

"It's the third movie, but the second book. It's the true sequel."

"That's great."

"Well, it's not great. It has its moments, but it's a bit too convoluted for me. Never really makes the impact the first one did."

"Thanks for that," Marv said, before finishing the coffee in his cup. "I think it's probably best if we were quiet for a while."

Something caught his attention in the churchyard. A movement beyond the gravestones, a fleeting tremor under the moonlight, although it might well have been his eyes playing tricks on him.

"Wait!" he said, his finger pointing towards the dark mass of trees at the back of the church grounds. "I saw something!"

"Where?" Connor asked, searching through the windscreen.

"Over by the trees."

"You sure?"

Marv didn't answer, but opened his door quietly and stepped out of the car. Connor followed his lead.

"I'll go through this gate," Marv whispered. "You go around and meet me round the back."

Connor nodded and disappeared into the dark mass of trees beyond the wall of the church as Marv scurried through the gate into the churchyard.

He weaved his way, cautiously through the gravestones, careful to avoid standing on the graves, cursing silently as he knocked over a vase of flowers.

He made his way to the corner of the church, keeping close to the building and listening as he went. At first it was just the breeze rustling through the trees and then he heard the scuff of a shoe on the tarmac. He sprung from behind the church and scared his partner half to death.

"Jesus!" Connor yelped.

"Did you see anybody?" Marv asked, confused.

"No. Just your ugly mug leaping out at me!"

Marv brushed by him, his eyes scrutinising the dark foliage at the back of the churchyard and then turned to the corner of the church that was missing the stone grotesque.

"Shit," said Marv.

"Four down," said Connor. "Eight to go."

EIGHT

Blake awoke, the sunlight hot on his face. He had fallen asleep the night before, fully clothed on the top of his bed, playing Tetris on his phone. He coughed and brushed the biscuit crumbs from his face and then the pillow, before farting himself to an upright position and stretching.

After realising he was running late to meet Olivia at the café, he quickly threw on some semi-fresh clothes and left the house, stopping only to grab an apple on his way out.

He hated being late. It only added to the catalogue of things stacking up in his life, designed to make him feel bad about himself… couldn't figure out what subjects to take, couldn't figure out what career path to embark upon, couldn't be arsed to write this or that essay… couldn't be arsed to drag himself out of bed in a morning. The list went on.

He knew it too. He knew full well that the apathetic part of himself was given to indolence, but he was often too lethargic to do anything about it. That was the thing with idleness, it was a difficult pit to clamber out of.

He made his way to the café, as briskly as was comfortable, occasionally looking at his watch, occasionally just enjoying the birdsong from the trees and bushes that lined his walk.

"Sorry, I'm late!" he said, upon opening the door and entering and checking his watch to check he was only twenty minutes late.

Olivia rolled her eyes at him. "Don't worry. It isn't the first time."

"I overslept."

"You do know you have an alarm on your phone, don't you?"

"I forgot to set it," he said, taking a seat opposite.

"Call Of Duty?" she asked.

"Some," he yielded. "I also went old school Tetris on my phone. I fell asleep with a pack of biscuits."

"It's crazy that you're still single," she said.

"Ha ha," he replied over-dramatically. "Did you end up going to The Griffin last night?"

"Yeah. Jim's new band was playing."

"What are they called, again?"

"Melted Clown Lunchbox," she replied, little in the way of expression in the delivery.

"Right. Any good?"

"No. It was a bit like being continuously mugged for forty minutes."

Blake laughed. "How is Jim, these days?"

"Not great, if the lyrics of the songs are anything to go by."

"Bit dark, were they?"

40

"The one's I could understand were, yeah," Olivia laughed too. "He screamed most of them though and the last song was just him crying to guitar feedback."

"It sounds pioneering," Blake smiled.

"It would do, to someone who wasn't there. To me, it was just the best part of an hour that I won't be getting back."

Irene appeared from the kitchen and slowly made her way towards them.

"Morning, Irene," greeted Blake. "Just a 'coffee', please."

"There's a man in my bin," she replied, her voice as fragile as usual, but perhaps a little more bemused.

"Pardon?" Blake asked, unsure if he had heard her correctly.

"Outside, in the yard. There's a man in my bin."

"Okay," Blake replied, looking over at Olivia, to see if she looked as confused as he felt. She did.

He stood from the table and walked over to the kitchen, passing Irene as he went.

"I'll just take a look, shall I?"

"Thank you, dear," the old lady said, as he disappeared through the kitchen. Olivia stood too and followed her friend.

"I'm sure it's nothing," she said, putting a hand on the old woman's shoulder. "Better double-check though."

Blake walked to the kitchen window and peered out into the back yard, where a man was dusting himself down, next to the large, open bin.

He opened the kitchen door and stepped out into the yard.

"Excuse me!" he called, as the man quickly turned around. "Ven?"

"Ah, morning," Ven replied, relieved at seeing a familiar face.

"I thought you'd gone?"

"It's difficult to explain," he said, a little sheepishly.

"What are you doing in Irene's bin?"

41

"Again, it's a bit difficult to explain," he said, brushing bits from his trousers.

"Well try," said Olivia, stepping out into the yard, "because if you don't, I'm calling the police. This shit is just getting creepy now."

"Listen, I know it seems weird…" he began.

"It doesn't *seem* anything," she butted in. "It *is* weird. You can either talk to us or the police. Your choice."

Blake had always known Olivia was a very practical and logical person. She didn't suffer fools gladly, as they say, although she did suffer him. What he hadn't seen before was the level of grit now coming to the fore and he liked it, even if it did highlight his own shortcomings in that department.

"Fine," he eventually conceded, "but not out here," he added, nervously.

They ushered him into the café, via the kitchen, sitting at the back of the room, and asked Irene for a round of coffees.

"We're listening," Olivia prompted him.

"Okay. I work for… *used to* work for a company called Zenith." He paused for a moment, thinking of how best to tell it.

"What do they do?" asked Blake.

"I'm guessing not washing machines," said Olivia.

"I can't say exactly, but let's just call it 'course correction'."

"Course correction?" Blake asked, confused at the vagueness of the answer. "Are you a satnav?"

"It's just the best way to explain it," Ven said, defensively.

"Carry on," Olivia urged him.

"I had a crisis in confidence, shall we say…"

"A breakdown," Blake interjected.

"Whatever. I didn't agree with some of the decisions being made or some of the actions being implemented and so decided to leave."

"So you quit?" Olivia asked.

"Not in so many words." He looked out through the bay window to the street beyond, bathed in the morning sunshine. "It's not a company you can just leave. They're a bit more insistent that you're with them for life. Twenty-four/seven."

"You get days off though, right?" said Blake. "I mean, you can get them on employment law there."

"It's a little bit beyond all that," said Ven. "These are people that make their own rules."

"The government! I knew it!" he called out.

"I wish," came the man's reply.

"Higher than the government?" Olivia asked. "What's higher than the government?"

"Zenith is."

"Does the government know about them?" Blake asked.

"Not as such, and not officially, but certainly some at the top are in the know, to some degree at least."

"I'm getting Illuminati vibes," he said, as Irene shuffled in with a tray of drinks. Ven scoffed as Blake stood to take the tray from her and place it on the table. He thanked the old woman, before she returned to the kitchen.

"I suppose you think they're just a myth?" Blake said.

"No, they're real. They're just not what you think."

"I'm not sure what I think."

"They're more of a private club than anything else. Sure, they have influence. They're made up of very influential people, after all, but it's more of a forum for ideas than anything and besides, a few of the members are also aware of Zenith"

They all took a moment to sip at their drinks, Blake and Olivia taking a moment to process the information, as best as they could.

"Cold tea, yeah?" Blake said.

"Yep," Olivia said, pulling a face as she drank it.

"I thought you asked for coffee?" said Ven.

"I did. This is usual. It's fine."

"So," Olivia said, steering the conversation back on track. "Why were you in Irene's bin? We thought you'd left."

"I was about to leave, but I noticed some Bleachers hanging around…"

"Bleachers?" Olivia said.

"Yeah, they get sent in to clean up any 'mess' that's sometimes left behind. It's a nickname for the people that do the dirty work."

"And you saw some here in Chapel-on-the-Moss?" she asked.

"Yeah. I'm positive. They have a certain way about them."

"Are they still here?"

"I don't know. I stayed to backyards last night, trying to keep an eye out for them. I jumped in the bin for warmth and to stay out of the way and obviously fell asleep."

"I can't imagine sleeping in a bin," said Blake.

"It was just the cardboard recycling," Ven explained. "It actually makes for a reasonable insulator, especially in an enclosed environment."

"So, now what?" Olivia asked.

"I can't head out just yet," he said. "Not without being sure that they're gone. Hopefully they'll finish off their hunt today and leave."

He sounded genuine and she liked to think she was a good judge of character.

"If they're as determined as you've described, why would they leave empty-handed?" she asked.

"I'm hoping they conclude that I've already left the area." He took a drink of cold tea.

Hope was all he had.

NINE

Arthur sprinkled the contents of the watering can on to his carrots. The sun was doing them the world of good, but it was important to keep on top of the watering.

He shook the last few drops from the can and then walked back over to his shed, noticing the tall man strolling over to him.

Standing at well over six feet, the man wore black trousers and shoes, a red shirt and a black cotton jacket down to his knees. He had a shaved head and a heavy build.

"Hello?" Arthur greeted him, cautiously.

The man smiled and completed his walk to the shed before speaking.

"Good morning," he spoke, his voice softer than his appearance.

"Can I help you?" Arthur asked.

"Well, perhaps you can," the man replied, through a fake smile. "I'm looking for an old friend that I know came through the village yesterday. I wondered if you'd seen him."

He reached into his pocket and produced a piece of paper with a printed photograph on. He handed it over to the old man.

"Can't say we get that many folks passing through," Arthur said, taking the picture. "It's only a small village."

"Well, then I'm sure you'd remember him," the man smiled.

"Let me get my glasses," Arthur said. "I'm no good with close-ups. I can't see the hand in front of my face without them."

He hobbled into the shed, pulled the string for the light and waited for the bulb to buzz dangerously into life, leaving the stranger to look around the allotment, to the other plots, to Arthur's vegetables and deck chair and eventually to the crushed chip to the side of the paving slab.

He bent down and picked it up, casting a brief eye over it, before placing it in his pocket.

"No, can't say that I have," said Arthur, emerging from the shed with his glasses on.

"You're quite sure?" the man asked.

"As sure as I can be. I spend most of the day right here though, so unless he has more than a passing interest in vegetables, he'd most likely give the allotments a miss, I reckon."

"You could be right," said the man.

"You sure it was this village he came through? Only you got Lower Trout a little further on. That's got a bit more to it... pub, a couple of guesthouses, even got a fancy takeaway that does all that foreign food."

"I'll be sure to check," the man smiled again and turned and walked back towards the gate. He glanced back as he left the allotment before disappearing into the woods.

Arthur removed his glasses.

"Trouble ahead," he mumbled to himself.

TEN

Marv climbed into the passenger seat and put his belt on as the car moved away from his house.

"You manage to get a few hours sleep?" Connor asked his partner.

"Yeah. She woke me up getting dressed though, so I didn't quite get the lie-in that I wanted," Marv complained. "Right noisy cow, honestly. She closes the drawers like they've wronged her somehow and she's taking revenge."

"Well, at least you didn't wake up in a mood," Connor remarked, sarcastically.

It was a ten minute drive into the town of Middlesworth, a small town with a population of around fifteen to twenty thousand people. What it lacked in size, it more than made up for in character. There was a good deal of Tudor architecture still standing, white washed buildings with thick black wooden beams, twisted over time, along with many of the walls they supported, but quaint none-the-less.

It was still a decent town centre too, despite the decline in recent years. There was still a family butchers, an independent florist, an independent cards and occasions shop and a number of retail chains still clinging on, amongst the bookies and the charity shops.

The police station was opposite the library, before you got as far as all the shops. It was a two-storey office block, devoid of any interesting architectural features. They had built this place post-war with a budget in mind, cheap and functional.

They parked up and made their way into the building, slowly, knowing that their failed stakeout wouldn't have escaped the attention of the detective sergeant.

"She's going to be pissed off, isn't she?" Connor worried.

"When is she not?" Marv replied. "The last time that woman cracked a smile, I think they were still writing parts of the Bible."

They entered the building through the lobby, both nodding at the officer on reception, before walking through the double doors and up the stairs to the main offices.

Detective Sergeant Ellen Cole was, by pure happenchance, walking out of her office at the end of the long room, when she saw them.

"Ah, Eagle Eyes and the Stakeout Kid, I was wondering when you'd get here. I thought someone might have stolen you on your way in." She motioned for them to follow her into her office.

"I bet she's been waiting all morning to say that," Marv whispered to his partner, as they crossed the room.

They entered the office, Connor closing the door behind them, before being seated opposite their superior. Her stern blue eyes staring back at them, the lines on her mature face creased in disappointment.

"So then, what happened?" she asked, after an awkward few moments of silence.

The two men looked baffled, lost for anything to say.

"Okay, let me put it another way. How did the gargoyle you were watching get stolen while you were watching it?"

"It was a grotesque, ma'am," Marv corrected her.

"Excuse me?"

"It was a grotesque. Gargoyles are actually used to steer rainwater away from a building, like a funnel. Grotesques have no practical purpose."

"Like yourselves?" she asked.

Marv coughed a little to clear the embarrassment in his throat.

"We were parked pretty close to the church and didn't see anyone enter or leave, ma'am," Connor explained.

"And yet they must have done. Do you think that maybe they thought walking in and out of the churchyard by the front gate was a little bit too predictable?"

Marv gave a nod.

"Carrying a large stone statue too. Remind me, how big are the statues?"

"About two feet," said Marv.

"Must be quite heavy," she surmised.

"Yes, ma'am," they both said together.

"Might I suggest that you go down to the church and set up some camera equipment and maybe check for any alternative exit points? Aside from that, could you possibly find time to do some detective work and find some leads?"

"Yes, ma'am," again from them both in unison.

"You are both trained in criminal investigation techniques, aren't you?"

"Yes, ma'am."

"I thought I'd better check, because all evidence from my brief investigation leads to the contrary. Would you like me to put you down for some additional training?"

"No, ma'am."

"That will be all," she concluded.

The two detectives took their leave and made the long walk back through the desk-filled room and down the stairs to reception.

"Well, that was as lovely as ever," Marv said.

"I don't think we're top of her Christmas card list," Connor remarked, opening a door, heading for the technical support department.

"Let's just get the camera stuff and head back. The sooner we solve this, the sooner she'll leave us alone."

ELEVEN

"You should be safe coming this way," Blake said, as they walked by the side of the old brook. "Most people don't even know this path exists."

Ven could well believe it. Overgrown thorns had scratched at his legs for the last ten minutes. They seemed to make up most of the fauna that ran alongside the brook, broken only by the occasional patch of bluebells. Trees lined the brook too, in the throes of losing their blossom, but thick with life and heavily scented in the morning sun, they provided ample cover from prying eyes.

"So, this friend of yours..." Ven began.

"Mason" Blake interrupted.

"Yeah. You sure it's safe to stay at his? Ouch," he added, as the latest thorn snatched at him.

"It's his parent's farm, but he lives in an old barn at the bottom of the property, away from everyone else. It's the perfect place to hide out for a day or two. Ouch," he also added.

"You sure they'll be watching the roads in and out of the village?" Olivia asked, walking at the rear.

"It's standard protocol. Most footpaths too," Ven added. "I just need to keep my head down until they move on."

"So, there are a few people out there then?" she asked.

"I imagine a team of six to eight by now. I've been off-grid for around twenty-four hours and they will have been in the area for more than half of that. They'll be getting frustrated. Ouch. Hopefully they'll split up, move on to the next village and eventually leave this one completely."

They continued the trek, battling the thorns along the winding brook until they reached a narrow, tree-lined back road. The farm estate was a short distance along, on the other side of the road.

"It's just there." Blake pointed. "Through the gate. You can see Mason's barn through the trees."

Ven looked hard through the trees and made out an old stone building. It looked vaguely familiar and in need of repair at a glance.

"Okay." He thought for a second. "Blake, you head over first. Let's see if that draws out any agents. We'll give it a minute and then follow on."

"Thanks," Blake said, dryly.

"They're not looking for you, it'll be fine."

Blake did so, striding casually and confidently into the road. It took only twenty seconds or so to reach the gate on the other side and walk on to the property.

Ven and Olivia followed a moment later, Olivia feeling physically relieved once she stepped foot on Mason's land.

"All this sneaking around is making me nervous," she said.

"Thanks again, both of you," Ven said, noting her anxiety. "I appreciate your help."

"Well, don't thank us just yet," she smiled. "You haven't met Mason."

As they strolled up to the barn, Ven noted that it was ancient and in need of extensive repair. If the white dove on the roof had been any fatter, there was a good chance that the whole thing could have given way.

Blake knocked on the door. It was a distinct knock, one that Blake and Mason had worked out between them. Mason liked to know who he was answering the door to.

He eventually opened the door, spliff hanging from his mouth, his long dark hair in a pony-tail, his scrawny beard littered with crisps and ash.

"How's it going, man?" he asked, his pink eyes, warm and as manic as ever.

"Not bad," Blake replied.

"Hey, Liv," Mason added, seeing her standing behind Blake.

"Hi, Mason."

"Who's this?" he asked, staring at Ven.

"This is Ven," Blake introduced. "I need to ask you a favour."

"Better come in."

He opened the door wider and ushered them in, before closing the door behind them and following them through to the main room.

It wasn't exactly a living room. It was still essentially a barn. The stone walls were exposed and warped in places, no doubt suffering from a lack of decent mortar and the stone floor was

55

covered only by the occasional rug, with two poor excuses for settees and a coffee table that looked as if it had been fly-tipped into the room. There were several televisions and monitors in the corner, seemingly connected by a litter of wires, which looked dangerously exposed, and all connected to a number of computer towers, humming quietly to themselves.

The sweet smell of cannabis hung in the air, a visible haze warmed by the sun streaming in through the small windows.

"Okay," said Ven, sizing up the place.

"So, what can I do for you?" Mason asked his friend.

Blake didn't know where to begin. "It's kind of a long story, but the short of it is that Ven is on the run and needs to keep his head down. Just for a day or two. I was wondering if you'd be able to let him stay here?"

"On the run, eh?" Mason asked, turning his stoned gaze to the former agent.

Ven nodded.

"Who you running from, man?"

"Erm, not to go too much into it… government types," he replied.

"Well, I'm no fan of the government. Is it anything to do with all those lights in the woods last night?"

Ven thought for a moment before replying. "Erm…"

"What is it, man, UFOs or fae folk?"

"Er..." Ven was a bit confused now. "What are fae folk?" he asked.

"Fairies, man. Pixies and shit. Apparently, they really come alive at night." Mason was buzzing with enthusiasm on the topic, much as he had been with Blake, the night before.

"I wouldn't have thought…" Ven's sentence trailed off.

"Mason has a few interesting theories on unexplained phenomena," Blake explained.

"Fairies aren't what you think, man," Mason elaborated. "It's not all Tinkerbell blowing sparkle dust out of her arse and happy flying nymphs dossing about the place. They're actually pretty nasty. Bite your eyes out."

"Right," Ven acknowledged, with a somewhat bewildered expression on his face.

"Any chance of a brew?" Olivia asked, more to end the conversation than out of thirst.

"Oh, yeah. No worries," Mason said. "Park yourselves down. I'll bring some tea in."

He left the room to go into the ramshackle kitchen at the other end of the barn, leaving Ven to look at his two new companions with no small amount of worry.

"He's a bit eccentric," Blake confirmed.

"Really? I hadn't noticed," said Ven.

"Listen, it's out of the way."

"It's fine," Ven said, his hands up in submission.

"I can always check this evening if the road out is clear and text Mason to let him know." Blake looked at Olivia.

"And if not, I can always check again tomorrow morning," she added.

"Thankyou," Ven replied. "I mean it. This place might not be The Ritz, but it will do just fine."

"You might just have to put up with a few conspiracy theories for a while," Blake said, apologetically.

"I'm sure I've sat through worse," he replied.

A moment later, Mason returned with a pot of tea and four cups on an old metal tray.

"You can sit down, you know?" he said, placing the tray on the coffee table.

"So, you're okay with Ven staying for a bit?" Blake asked, sitting on the settee, next to Mason, as his friend poured the tea into the cups.

"Yeah, man. Help yourself to sugar," he added, pointing to an open pack of sugar with a rusty spoon sticking out of the top.

They all sat now, Ven taking a sip of his brew.

"Unusual taste," he said, reclining into the low settee, next to Olivia.

"It's herbal."

TWELVE

Marv opened the boot of the car and perused the camera equipment.

"I hope you've got an idea of how to set all this up," he said, as his partner joined him at the rear of the car.

"I think it's fairly straight forward," Connor replied. "We shouldn't need all of it. We only need to stick one camera looking at the remaining statues and maybe one taking in the back of the churchyard."

"Sounds like you know what you're doing. Make sure you don't miss anywhere or the troll will cross us off more than just her Christmas list!"

As Connor tinkered with the equipment in the boot, Marv noticed a tall man, dressed in black walking slowly towards them. He was a lean man with a shaven head, looking towards their car as he neared.

"You alright?" Marv called, as the man approached closer.

The man completed his walk before responding.

"Hello," he smiled.

"Can we help you?" Marv asked.

"Perhaps," he replied. "I'm looking for a friend of mine. He would have travelled through this way. I wonder if you've seen him?"

The man produced a picture and handed it to Marv.

"Is he missing?" Marv asked.

"No, he's just an old friend," the tall man smiled back.

"I'm just wondering why you happen to have a photo of your old friend printed out on a piece of paper?" Marv said, a little confused.

"His mother said he had come this way and gave me the picture, as I haven't seen him in quite a few years. He's changed a bit." The man's smile wavered slightly.

"Could his mother not just give you his phone number?" Connor asked, looking up from the boot.

"She didn't know it," the man replied, after a short pause.

"Close family, yeah?" Marv smiled.

"I just wondered if you'd seen him," said the man, taking the picture back and folding it, before putting it in his pocket.

"No. Afraid not," Marv said.

"Very well. Good day," said the man, walking away from them again.

"Christ, there's some strange folks about these days," Marv said, watching the man walk away.

"You're one of them," Connor laughed.

"He looked like he should have been swiping goats off a bridge!"

"Are you helping with this?" Connor asked.

"I wasn't planning on it, but if you're going to get all pissy, I'll help you carry some of it over," Marv jested.

"You're too kind."

THIRTEEN

They were all sat, slumped into the settees, listening intently to Mason as he continued to tell his story.

"Then what happened?" asked Ven.

"Well, then the police came and cordoned off the area. They ordered everybody out of there, but my friends said they'd already seen what was in the cave."

"What did they see?" Olivia asked, her mouth open, eyes pink with heavy lids, hanging on Mason's words.

"They said it was half-crocodile and half man," Mason concluded.

Blake burst out laughing. "No way!"

"Seriously," Mason confirmed, lighting the spliff from the ashtray.

Ven laughed too. "I think that's probably incorrect."

"Nah, that's what they said," Mason smiled, blowing out a huge cloud of scented smoke. "Some kind of lizard guy. Teeth like knives."

Olivia laughed along with Blake and Ven now, ultimately catching her breath and looking accusingly at the teapot.

"Did that tea have weed in it?" she asked.

"Yeah," Mason replied, quite innocently. "I always make weed tea."

"Ah, now it makes sense that I'm listening to your stories," Blake chuckled.

"Well, yeah," Mason smiled. "You're expanding your mind, allowing yourself to open up to new possibilities."

"That's what you meant when you said 'herbal' tea?" said Ven, a little annoyed at having been side-stepped into getting high, but high nonetheless and reasonably cheerful about it, if he was being honest with himself.

"Man, everybody seemed pretty stressed out. You're on the run…"

"So you might think I'd want my wits about me?" Ven said, but there was no sting in the remark. He was enjoying the high, regardless of what his common sense was saying. Besides, it wasn't like he was drunk and staggering around with some unfathomable false bravado, he was just mellow and in a better mood. He still felt more than capable of functioning should the need arise for him to flee.

"You still have your wits about you, man," Mason assured him. "The tea just brought you down a notch. Everybody's chilled and telling stories. Well, I suppose I'm the only one telling stories," he added.

"Actually, I have a story too," Blake began.

"Really?" Olivia asked. "Sounds ominous."

"A couple of years ago, I was up in the attic, looking for some of my dad's old computer games... really old Commodore stuff..."

"Flashback for the Amiga?" Mason interrupted.

"Yes!" Blake called out, emphatic in his confirmation. "That was the exact game!"

"Great game, man," Mason nodded, smiling at the distant, half-baked memory of playing it at some time or another.

"Never mind that," Olivia said. "What happened in the attic?"

"I saw a ghost," he said, leaving a pause for effect. "I mean, I think I saw a ghost. I turned the light on and I saw a shadow figure move to the corner of the attic, behind a stack of boxes."

"Could it have been *your* shadow?" Olivia smiled, knowingly.

"I suppose we'll never know," he shrugged.

"I think I know," she said.

"Did you follow it?" Mason asked.

"No," he replied, to an audience of unimpressed faces.

"Worst story ever, man," Mason laughed.

"Yeah, that was poor," Ven agreed.

"What about you, Mr On The Run?" Mason said, turning to Ven. "I bet you have some stories."

"More than I care to remember," he said. "I'm not at liberty to repeat any of them though."

"That sucks," said Mason.

"I don't think you have to be quite so allegiant to whatever ballbag company you worked for now that they're trying to get you," Olivia said. "I'd like to hear a story or two."

"Yeah, I think you owe us a story," Blake said, piling on the pressure.

"Okay," Ven said, sitting forward a little as Mason handed him the joint. He took it without thinking and continued. "I suppose I could tell one or two."

"That's it, man," Mason grinned. "Don't wet the roach."

"There was this one time, when I was out on a job," he started. "It was a regular job really, straight forward course correction, I should have been in and out. I had to get a file from out of a guy's desk and destroy it…" he took a drag of the joint and offered it to Blake first and then Olivia, and then back to Mason after they had politely declined.

"It was a sunny day in France, out in the countryside, beautiful estate, beautiful house, minimal security too for this kind of job. Anyway, I'm in the study and I've gotten into the desk drawer, checking the file to make sure I've got the right one and I realise this huge dog is just sat there staring at me. Huge, big jowls, mean eyes, muscles like it was living on press-ups and pedigree steroids."

Blake could picture the type of dog; he'd been chased by one as a teenager and that kind of thing stuck with you.

"So, I'm moving very slowly, carefully putting the file in my backpack and putting it back on, thinking to myself, 'how the hell am I getting out of here', because the dog's sitting in the doorway."

Mason discovered part of a cornflake in his beard and ate it, only momentarily distracted. He took another drag on the spliff as Ven continued.

"All of a sudden, out of nowhere, a white cat ran by me, out of the room and the dog ran after it. I just walked out of there the same way I got in. That was Fate," he added, with no small amount of gravitas.

"A cat saved your life, man," Mason said, through a plume of cannabis.

"Fate saved my life," he corrected. "That was a turning point," he added, reflectively.

"That was a pretty good story, but I'm sure you've got better," Blake said, egging the man on. "I think you're holding out on us."

"Okay. There was the time I was in the Houses of Parliament, destroying some documents that were meant for China," he ventured.

"Jesus, man. What the hell do you do, exactly?" Mason asked.

There was a knock on the door, chilling the room into a stoned silence.

"It's probably my mum," Mason assured them. "She still does my washing," he added.

"Doesn't she know the special knock?" Blake asked.

"She does, but she refuses to use it 'cos she's a dick."

"And if it isn't your mum?" Ven asked.

"Should we hide?" Blake asked, looking at Ven as he said it, but happy for anyone to answer.

Ven looked around the place, his eyes settling on some old crates and unpacked boxes at the back of the room. He stood and moved over to them. Blake and Olivia watched as he went.

"We don't need to hide," Olivia said. "Nobody's after us."

"Oh yeah," Blake sighed. "I think I'm a bit stoned."

Mason wandered out of the room and paused for a second or two before opening the front door.

"Hello?" he said, upon being faced with a tall, smart-looking man with a shaved head.

"Hello," the man smiled back. "Sorry to bother you. I was just wondering if you had seen this man?"

Mason looked around at the surrounding trees, checking to see if the man was alone, as he was handed a piece of paper with a picture of Ven printed on it.

"No, why?" Mason asked.

"He's a very dangerous individual," said the man, eerily still smiling.

66

"He doesn't look it," Mason said, handing the picture back.

"Well, appearances can be deceiving."

"That's true," Mason smiled. "You look pretty menacing yourself," he chuckled, trying to keep the barb light, but wanting to make it all the same. He enjoyed pushing the buttons of authoritative figures.

"I get that a lot," the man said. "It's my height."

"If you say so, man," Mason replied. "Sorry, I couldn't be more help."

"Oh, you've been very helpful," the man said, before turning and walking away from the building.

Mason closed the door and walked back into the room.

"Man, that was one strange individual," he said, lighting up the end of a joint from the ashtray.

"Was he after Ven?" Blake asked.

"Yeah," Mason nodded.

"Shit," said Ven, rising from behind the clutter at the back of the room.

"I didn't tell him anything," Mason said, attempting to allay any fears his new friend might have.

"Bleachers are extremely good at reading people. They're bred for it."

"Bleachers?" Mason said, puzzled.

"They clean up the mess," Blake explained. "Don't they?" he added, looking back at Ven.

"This might be a good thing," Olivia said. "We're on the outskirts of the village here, so maybe it means that they're close to moving on?"

Ven thought for a moment. "Maybe."

"Why don't I make another brew?" Mason suggested.

"Coffee," said Ven, sternly. "And just coffee this time," he added, determined to stay alert.

67

FOURTEEN

"Ah, detectives," said the vicar. "I'm Reverend Hopewick... Simon," he said, approaching the pair, as they stood by the front pew.

"I'm Detective Weaving," said Marv, "and this is Detective Raines."

The vicar was a short, portly man in his mid-fifties, with a rapidly receding hairline and a bushy greying beard. He was a little eccentric, but most people who met him seemed to take to him.

"How are you getting on?" he asked.

"We've finished putting the cameras out there, so fingers crossed we'll catch the bastard this time round," said Marv, before remembering where he was. "Oh, sorry, Reverend..."

"Oh, you're quite alright, don't apologise," the vicar insisted. "I swear myself, sometimes. I said 'bollocks' last week."

The detectives looked back at him with mildly surprised expressions.

"Right," said Marv.

"Not out loud, of course. I wouldn't say 'bollocks' out loud, certainly not in front of anyone."

"Right," Marv repeated.

"So, the cameras are up, are they?" he said, changing the subject.

"Yeah, so we're all done for now," said Marv. "But we'll be back later to keep watch."

"Splendid. Did you want a spot of tea before you go?" he asked. "I'm just about to have a scone too, if you'd like one?"

"Thanks anyway, but we've got a long night ahead of us and we're going to go home and get a few hours sleep first."

"Good thinking. I'll probably nod off myself after the scone. I say nod off... I think it's technically a short coma. I'm diabetic, you see"

"Right," said Marv, again.

"It's always fine as long as I wake up for when the parishioners get here," he laughed. "Plenty more of them at the minute too, with all this talk of the spectre."

"Spectre?" Connor asked.

"Yes. 'The phantom of the chapel', they're calling it."

"Really?"

"It's a bit silly, I suppose, but you know what people are like, Detective," the vicar said, rolling his eyes. "The younger ones are especially captivated. Well, they let their imaginations run wild. Still, numbers are up, which is nice."

"People can't resist a ghost story, can they?" Marv smiled.

69

"It would seem not," the vicar agreed. "Well, all the best for tonight and thanks again."

They bid their farewell and left the church, walking back out into the afternoon sunshine.

"He did say 'bollocks' out loud," said Connor.

FIFTEEN

Mason handed Olivia and Ven a bowl of mashed potato and baked beans each.

"Best thing ever," he said, disappearing back into the kitchen to get Blake's and his own.

Ven eyed the bowl curiously.

"Gordon Ramsey, eat your heart out," Olivia said.

Mason returned, passing a bowl to Blake and then sitting on the settee, to tuck into his own. He first reached into his shirt pocket and pulled out a sachet of ketchup.

"I won't ask," said Olivia, looking on as he squirted the contents over the mash.

"Best thing ever," he repeated, before spooning a mouthful into his face.

"Pretty good, actually," Ven said, upon his first mouthful.

"I reckon this would go perfectly with a tuna steak," said Blake, tucking in.

"Why ruin it?" asked Olivia.

"Don't you like tuna?"

"I can't eat anything with a face," she replied.

"I did not know that about you," said Blake, surprised. "How come you never said?"

"You never asked."

"I'm similar," said Mason. "Except, I can't eat anything with feet."

"With feet?" Blake puzzled.

"Yeah, man. Feet are gross. Any feet. It's making me feel ill just talking about them."

It didn't take long for them to finish their five-star gourmet cuisine and for the chat to return to matters at hand.

"So, Ven, where will you go?" Olivia asked.

"There's a place I've heard about, where I should be safe," he replied.

"Is it far?" Mason asked.

"Distance doesn't really come into it."

"Oh, that sounds… ambiguous." It was Blake's turn to ask a question. "Is it on a map?"

"Not on a regular map," Ven replied, as evasive as ever.

"I bet I could find it," said Mason, seeming quite sure of himself.

"I doubt it," said Ven.

"I specialise in the unknown," Mason assured him.

"I'll back him up on that one," Blake smiled. "If there's a conspiracy, secret agenda, buried information… Mason is your man."

"You do seem to have a rather… extravagant set-up," Ven said, giving Mason's computer area a look over and by 'extravagant' he meant untidy.

"State-of-the-art, man," he said, proudly. "I built it myself."

"It looks home-made," Ven agreed.

"You know, I can hack into pretty much anywhere with this. It also has a scrambling unit so nothing can get traced back to me."

"It sounds great," Ven humoured him.

"I once got into the Supermarket's system to see if there was a particular reason why they had put the tins of beans up by eight percent."

He was met with unaffected stares.

"It was three percent above inflation," he said, defensively.

"I think I remember you telling me about that," said Blake. "You took the whole thing pretty hard."

"Yeah, man. It took me around three days to get to the bottom of it, but I got answers!"

"Was it some dastardly plot to extort hard-earned money from the masses?" Olivia asked, smiling.

"No. Turns out they were just making up for the fact that they hadn't put the beans up for three years straight and couldn't soak up the cost increases anymore."

"That's… impressive," Ven said, struggling for the right word.

"Alright, I guess that was a poor example, but the point is that I got to the bottom of it."

"You did," Ven agreed. "Listen, if I needed to find it, I'd have you look, but I don't, because I already know where it is."

"Is that why these guys are chasing you?" Mason asked.

"That might be part of it," he sighed. "Let's just say I had a change of heart with regards to my employment. I became

73

aware of the truth and made a choice about which side I wanted to be on."

"The truth about what?" Blake asked, placing his empty bowl on the table.

"The truth about everything," he replied, profoundly.

"Vague much?" said Olivia.

"I can't go into detail about…"

"Because we're better off not knowing, blah, blah, blah…" Olivia cut him off. "Were you better off not knowing?"

Ven thought for a moment. "That's different."

"Is it?" she asked. "Seems like you just want it to be different."

"I'm trying to protect you. The less you know, the safer you are."

"And how safe are we, exactly?" she pressed on.

"How do you mean?"

"Well, we've already stuck our neck out for you. If these people find out we've helped you, I'd like to know what the consequences will be."

"You'll be seen as unimportant," Ven replied, eventually.

"And that means we're safe, does it? Or does that mean we're expendable?"

Blake was looking at Olivia now. She was like a dog with a bone, unable to let it go and it was impressive. He imagined she would be a great political interviewer. Perhaps that was a career she should entertain. He made a mental note to tell her at some point.

"It means they'll be too busy looking for me to pay you any mind."

"Well, I still think you owe us a bit more clarity," she said.

"As I've said already, I work for a company called Zenith. They specialise in course correction. Recently I discovered some things about the company I didn't like and so I decided to leave."

Mason was all ears, hearing this for the first time. "What's course correction?" he asked.

"Complicated," came the reply.

"Oh, that's much clearer," he said.

"Unfortunately, Zenith isn't the sort of company you can just leave and so they're trying to get me back."

"What will they do if they get you back?" asked Blake.

"I'm not sure," he shrugged. "Nobody's ever left before."

"Ever?" Blake asked, stunned at such a huge level of employee retention.

"Not that I know of, although that's not to say it hasn't happened and I just don't know about it, I suppose."

"Every time we ask questions, we end up with more questions," Olivia remarked, before standing and announcing she was going to the bathroom.

"I think you should come clean, man," said Mason, picking up a short stub out of the ashtray and lighting it.

"I wish it was that easy," Ven said, doodling on a piece of paper.

SIXTEEN

"Did you get any sleep or did you end up going back to the station?" asked Marv, sitting in the passenger seat and closing the car door.

"I went to the station," said Connor.

"I thought you would. Did you manage to check the files for any potential suspects?"

"I did a run on teenagers with any related priors in the Chapel-on-the-Moss area," Connor replied, as the car pulled away from the kerb.

"And?"

"And it's a very small area and apart from a kid with a few warnings for cannabis, there's nothing."

"Do you think it could be some kind of stoner prank?" Marv asked.

"I'm just not sure it's very funny as far as pranks go," said Connor, after a moment of deep thought.

"Yeah, but you're not a stoner."

"Listen, I've smoked pot before and it didn't make me want to go out and steal ridiculously heavy stone gargoyles."

"Grotesques."

"Whatever. It made me want to stay sat on my arse all night eating cheesy snacks."

"When did you smoke pot?" asked Marv, playfully.

"Never mind that. I just think it's too much effort for a stoner."

"So you don't think its kids doing this?"

"Not stoned ones," he said, stopping at a set of traffic lights.

The sky was a dark blue now, as they looked out of the car windscreen. Only a strip of light blue remained over a partly obscured horizon, peppered with the occasional orange and pink cloud.

"What about neighbouring villages?" Marv asked, as the lights turned green.

"There was a teenager in Lower Trout that once got drunk and made a giant fort out of everybody's wheelie bins."

"I think he might be worth putting on the 'maybe' list," said Marv.

"Well, I thought that, but it was going on four years ago and the guy is nearly twenty now and training to be an architect."

"Could be using the statues as inspiration?" said Marv, trying to think outside the box.

"I think we might be clutching at straws on that one."

"Fair enough."

As they drove out of the town, the road was at first flanked by fields and four or five minutes later by woodland, as they headed for Chapel-on-the-Moss.

77

"Did you just see some blue lights over in the woods?" Marv asked.

"Where?" Connor asked, looking to the woods at the side of the road.

"No, not here. The woods on the horizon, over there." He pointed ahead.

"No," Connor said. "What did it look like?"

"Blue lights," Marv repeated, unhelpfully.

"Were they flashing, were they moving...?"

"They were moving, a handful of them and then they just stopped."

"You want to go and check them out?" Connor asked.

Marv thought for a moment. He didn't want to be late for the stakeout; didn't want another statue to be stolen before they even got there! He wasn't sure his immediate career could withstand such a knock, dented as it was already, certainly in the eyes of the troll in charge.

"Yeah," he eventually decided. '*What career?*' he thought.

SEVENTEEN

They had spent a good deal of the evening talking about everything and nothing, from baked beans to global cabals and chihuahuas to the inventions that shaped the world.

Mason had at one point gone off on a tangent, trying to explain how the number eleven kept cropping up at significant points in his life.

Blake had argued that this was down to coincidence and that something had possibly happened once or twice and then subsequent occurrences had been attributed retrospectively to suit the narrative, albeit subconsciously.

Ven had simply shrugged, not wanting to commit to the story, but both Blake and Olivia noticed that it looked like the man had his own ideas on the subject.

Olivia grabbed her bag from the side of the settee and joined Blake at the front door.

"Thanks for the hospitality, Mason," Olivia said.

"No worries," he replied from behind a plume of smoke on the sofa.

"And thanks for giving Ven a place to keep his head down," Blake added.

"Any time, man."

"We'll keep to the main road on the way back," he said, looking at Ven now. "I'll text Mason if it's clear."

"Thanks," he replied. "And thanks again, all of you, for the help."

"No problem," said Blake, opening the front door and stepping out into the darkening evening.

No sooner than Olivia had closed the front door behind them, two figures, dressed in black flanked them both.

Blake felt the needle enter his neck, but before he could even let out a yelp, he felt numb and then everything blurred into blackness and he was out.

Olivia slumped to the ground next to him.

Inside, they were none the wiser.

"If you want, I can make another brew?" said Mason.

"I'll be fine," replied Ven, choosing to be cautious after the first time round.

"So, this Zenith outfit," Mason began. "They sound like a bunch of dicks, man."

"That's pretty much the sum of it," Ven agreed.

"How come you ended up working for them in the first place?"

"I always just assumed I was in the right place at the right time," he said. "Now I know even that was a lie."

Mason stubbed out the spliff in the ashtray and blew the smoke out into the room, now lit only by a small lamp near the computers.

"At first, I thought it was a great job," Ven continued. "It was exciting, I got to travel to a lot of different places and a lot of the jobs seemed harmless enough. I suppose as a rookie I never really got handed any of the bigger stuff and when the work got more..." he thought for the right word, "extreme, I just kind of justified it somehow."

He let out a big sigh and rubbed at the strain behind his eyes.

"You sure you don't want a brew?" Mason asked.

Ven laughed. "I wish that would help," he said, before noticing a stirring within the shadows of the kitchen area, beyond the short corridor that joined it to the main room.

There was no time to react.

The Bleachers walked slowly out of the shadows, three of them... tall, dressed in black jackets, red shirts, shaven heads... smiling.

Mason froze, perhaps questioning the reality of the situation, given how high he was.

"Woah, man. Triplets."

They ignored him, keeping their focus on Ven, sat on the opposite settee.

"I have to admit, I thought I'd get further than this," Ven said, with disappointment.

"Vitmyre was beginning to grow concerned," one of the Bleachers began, his voice overly soft, for his size and the situation. "It's not often one of his flock goes astray."

"There's so many of us that I didn't think he'd miss me," Ven said. "How is the old bastard?"

81

"I imagine he'll be much better for us having found you." The Bleacher looked over to Mason, who was still looking on in stoned silence. "Who is your friend?"

"I'm Mason," he said, slowly snapping out of it and beginning to take stock of the situation. "I don't know what's going on, but I imagine it would all sound much better over a brew."

The Bleacher looked back over at Ven. "Really? You're enlisting stoned teenagers to your cause?"

"There is no cause," he replied. "I've enlisted no-one. I was just lying low for the day."

"No cause? You expect us to believe that?"

"I don't really give a rat's tit what you believe, it's the truth. I'm not trying to start anything here. I'm trying to walk away. Haven't you heard of retirement?"

"I'm vaguely familiar with it. As I understand it, it's something people do before dying," came the reply.

"I don't know what's going on here, but maybe the guy just wants a few days off, man," said Mason. "I'm getting a strong corporate vibe from you fellas and maybe you've been working him too hard."

The three stared back at him, smiles still etched on to their pasty faces.

"And aside from that, you're beginning to really arsehole my buzz," Mason continued. "I'd appreciate it if you just left."

"We certainly don't intend to stay," the Bleacher replied.

One of the Bleachers approached Mason, grabbing him by the arm and lifting him, with ease, off the settee.

"Get off me, man!" he protested, but before he could shrug the man off, the needle slid into his neck and a moment later he slumped back to the settee, unconscious.

Ven stood.

"I'm ready to go," he said. "You don't need the injection."

"Who said anything about need?" the Bleacher replied, sticking the needle into Ven's neck.

One of the Bleachers caught him before he could fall to the floor and threw him over his shoulder, then walked out of the barn and into the near darkness. Only the darkness was now broken by headlights, as the car pulled up next to the barn.

Both detectives stepped out of the car, closing the doors behind them, staring at the men caught in the beams of the headlights.

"Does somebody want to tell me what's going on?" asked Marv.

THE HALF KNOWING

EIGHTEEN

The Sun was warm on his face.

He stirred and rolled over and whatever dream he was in slowly surrendered to reality.

He opened his eyes and realised that his pillow was another person.

Blake shot upright and looked at Olivia, though she remained asleep and snoring on the settee.

He looked over to see Mason asleep on the floor and two men that he had never seen before, asleep on the other settee.

'That must have been a hectic night' he thought, rubbing at his temples as the headache kicked in.

He had of course had hangovers before, but this one seemed particularly heavy. So heavy that he couldn't even remember drinking anything. He tried hard to recall where he had been but nothing came back to him and the effort of thinking was making him feel worse. In any case, he assumed it was The Griffin in Middlesworth, as they very rarely went anywhere else.

Olivia stirred next to him; no doubt awoken by Blake's movements.

"Morning?" she said, although it sounded like a question and came from a face that looked every bit as confused as he felt.

She sat up to showcase a crease down one side of her face, from the seam on the cushion.

"Morning," Blake replied.

"Did we get drunk?" she asked.

"I think we must have done. My head feels like a jar of elephant farts."

"Who are they?" she asked, glancing over to the other settee.

"No idea, but I think I'm going to be sick," he replied, standing and hurrying to the front door.

He had managed to grab the handle of the door when the sick filled his mouth. He tried to slap his other hand over the inevitable, but the force of it was too strong to contain and the sick shot out through the gaps in his fingers as he flung the door open and lunged forward, like an Olympic sprinter trying desperately to cross the line in a photo finish.

The rest of the outpouring continued on to the ground in front of him as he knelt, doubled over, heaving and spitting for all the morning to see.

Olivia also raced quickly to the door, unleashing her own vomit to the world.

It landed on Blake's shoulder, some of it in his hair and ear, warm and stinking.

"Oh, Jesus," he cried.

"I'm so sorr…" she mumbled, before being sick again, some of it splattering down her own arm, as she too knelt on the ground next to him.

Blake heaved out another pile.

"I'm never drinking again," he said, still thinking about Olivia's sick trickling down the side of his head. That made him heave again, although little more came up.

Mason staggered into the kitchen and in passing the front door, noticed his friends on all fours on the ground outside.

The warm stench of fresh vomit filled his nostrils. "For Christ's sake…" he muttered before being sick on to the pots in the sink, filling the bowls with used beans and mash.

He stared down at the state in front of him, and upon seeing a few readily identifiable beans, decided that he needed to chew his food more.

"Mason?" Blake called, hearing the heaves from inside.

"Yeah?"

"You alright?"

"Not really," he replied, head still firmly over the sink. "Were we drinking? I don't even remember going out."

"Nor me," he said, spitting away the tendrils of vomit and wiping his mouth with the back of his hand.

Blake took a deep breath of morning air and exhaled slowly, trying to push his body into a moment of calm. He looked over to Olivia, who was doing the same.

She looked at the sick on her arm and shook her head slowly, struggling to find any words to relay her current emotions. There weren't any and so she remained quiet.

"You got sick in my ear," said Blake, eventually.

"I'm so sorry," she said.

"Mason, please tell me you've got a hose pipe or something," Blake begged.

"Just down the side of the barn," he said, looking up from the pots.

"I think I'll need to borrow a clean top as well," he added, getting to his feet and tottering along the trunk of the building.

"You might want to get a couple of buckets too," Olivia added, "for your friends, when they wake up."

"They're not my friends," Mason replied. "I thought they were with you."

He left the comfort of the kitchen sink and grabbed the mop bucket from the side of the fridge, leaving the mop where it was.

He ambled slowly into the main room, not wanting to upset his already tender equilibrium.

Both men were beginning to come round and so he put the bucket down in front of the settee, before returning to the kitchen to grab a carton of orange juice and five assorted receptacles on a tray.

As he returned, he noted that one man was awake and sitting up, sporting a blank expression.

"Morning," greeted Mason.

"Morning?" said Connor, confused and casting a glance to Marv, as he struggled to open his eyes.

Mason poured the orange juice into the cups and glasses, before taking a mug and downing its contents in one. "Orange juice there," he nodded and burped.

Marv sat upright, too quickly for his own balance to catch up and had to close his eyes whilst his brain made the adjustment.

"What...?" he started.

"Guys, I'm guessing it was a good night, but some of us are having a rough and confusing morning," Mason said. "So, don't think me rude when I ask this. Who are you?"

"I'm Connor," he said, slowly, still trying to take stock of what was happening. "This is er... Marv."

"So, were we all at a party or something?" Mason asked, picking up the carton and finishing the last dregs.

"I doubt that," said Marv, finally opening his eyes and allowing the day to filter in.

"Did we meet at The Griffin, then?"

"The student place in town?" Connor asked.

"Yeah," said Mason.

"I doubt that too," said Marv.

"Then, why are you in my house?" It was a blunt question, but one that Mason felt needed asking.

Connor and Marv looked at each other, each of them united in confusion.

They both stood and made their way quickly to the front door.

Mason heard them emptying their stomachs on to the already soiled ground outside.

Olivia was hosing Blake down at the side of the barn, having hosed down her own arm first. She glanced back at the two strangers as they finished their emissions.

"Anyone need the hose?" she asked, as Blake stood.

"It's definitely out of my ear, isn't it?" he asked.

Five minutes later, they were all back in the main room, Marv and Connor on one settee, Blake and Olivia on the other and Mason sat, cross-legged on the floor facing them.

They all nursed cups of coffee and they all felt incredibly confused.

"What's the last thing you remember?" Blake asked Olivia.

89

"I'm not sure." She thought for a moment. "I think we were at Irene's Kitchen?" It wasn't a confident statement, but more of a wild stab in the dark based on a half-remembered memory, that may or may not have been a dream.

"I seem to remember that," agreed Blake. "That sounds like something that probably happened."

"So, did we come round here first and then go out?" Olivia asked.

The two of them looked at Mason, as he reached for his rolling papers.

"I think you must have done," he nodded. "I'm assuming I made mashed potatoes and beans before we left and judging by the amount of pots in the sink, it wasn't just me that had some."

"Are you rolling what I think you're rolling?" asked Marv.

"Yeah, man," Mason smiled. "It's new stuff. Should definitely help blow the cobwebs away."

"You can't do that," Marv said, placing his mug of coffee down on to the coffee table.

"Why not?"

"We're police detectives."

There was a stunned silence as the new information settled on the room.

"Shit," said Mason.

"What are you doing here?" asked Olivia.

"I've got absolutely no idea," said Marv. "I remember getting some camera equipment…"

"We installed it at the church," said Connor.

"That's right. Then I went home and went to sleep?"

"We were supposed to be keeping watch!" remembered Connor.

"Shit," Marv said, the realisation slowly dawning on him. "I think it's safe to say that probably didn't happen. Cole's going to be pissed."

"Didn't you see some lights?" Connor half-remembered.

"Oh, yeah!"

"Aliens, man," said Mason.

"What?" asked Marv.

"Alien abduction. That would explain the lights and the time-loss."

They looked at him blankly.

"Didn't you see some lights the other night?" Blake asked.

"Yeah, man. I thought they were fae folk, but this is sounding a lot more like aliens. I'd bet money on it. Do you feel like you've been probed?"

The stares back told Mason to err on the side of caution.

"There will be a perfectly normal explanation for this," Marv said.

"Such as?" Mason asked.

They didn't answer. They just sat for a moment and finished their coffee.

"Let's go and check the church," Marv said, as they both stood.

Connor handed Blake a card.

"This is my number. If you remember anything, give me a call."

"Thanks," he said.

They closed the door behind them and as soon as he heard the car drive away, Mason finished rolling the joint.

"Why would we invite two police detectives back?" asked Olivia.

"We wouldn't," said Mason, lighting his smoke and flipping the screen up on his laptop.

91

"I think… I think there was someone else," said Blake.

"Who?" said Olivia, placing her cup on the table.

"I'm not sure. Didn't we meet a guy the other day… on the way to…"

"Er, guys," Mason interrupted, his eyes fixed on his screen. "I think I just found something."

NINETEEN

The drive to the church seemed to last much longer than the five or six minutes it actually took.

The two detectives were still dazed and struggling to remember the exact details of the evening and certainly anything after seeing the lights.

"Do you think there's any chance that Cole is going to accept the story about the lights?" asked Connor, doing his best to pay attention to the road.

"I think there's more chance of Elvis being found alive, taking a shit on your toilet," replied Marv. "But don't worry, because there's no chance that we're going to mention the lights to her."

"Seems sensible," he agreed.

"With any luck, nothing happened at the church and the statues are all still there."

"I don't feel very lucky at the moment," Connor said. "I feel like you ran over my head."

"If another statue has gone, at least we left the cameras up and running, so we just go through the footage."

"We'd still have to explain why we simply continued to watch the footage and didn't give chase…"

"Well, let's not get ahead of ourselves just yet," Marv said. "We'll cross that bridge if we come to it."

"What *did* happen last night?" the younger man asked.

"We definitely didn't go out drinking, I know that much. Besides, it's been over a decade since I was able to go out and drink enough to forget everything… and I've really tried."

"You don't think it's…"

"What?"

"You don't think its aliens, do you?" Connor asked, tentatively, not wanting to sound foolish, but realising that it couldn't sound any other way.

"Of course not," Marv scoffed. "There'll be a perfectly logical explanation for it. Maybe we were drugged?"

"Why would anybody drug us?"

Marv thought for a moment. They wouldn't, was the conclusion he came to, but what were the alternative conclusions? Little green men? Faeries? Goblins? Where did you even draw the line with that kind of thinking? Are aliens really any more likely than the others?

"Maybe the 'dude' drugged us… the guy with the weed," Marv eventually said, but he knew he was reaching.

"He seemed like the last person who would want a pair of detectives over for a nightcap."

"Well, something's not right there," he said. "Let's check the footage at the church and pop back to the barn afterwards. Maybe there's something we've missed."

TWENTY

The three of them looked at the screen on the laptop, confused at what they were seeing.

Stuck to the screen was what appeared to be a crudely drawn map. It had been hastily doodled in biro on to the back of an old utility bill.

"What is it?" asked Blake.

"Looks like a map," said Mason, removing the piece of paper from the screen and studying it closely.

"Of where?" asked Olivia.

"I don't know," replied Mason. "It's a bit shit."

The three of them regarded the map.

Aside from a doodle of a tree with a tyre swing and the words 'find me', it was unfathomable. None of the other boxes or dotted lines looked like familiar routes or buildings at all.

"Do you think one of us did it, last night?" asked Olivia.

"Why would we?" asked Blake.

"Maybe it was some kind of game?" Mason said. "Like a treasure hunt."

"Aren't we a bit old for treasure hunts?" asked Olivia, tying her hair back into a ponytail, in a hope that tidying her hair might somehow restore tidiness to the inside of her head.

"Depends on the treasure," Mason smiled.

"Well, if it's one of us that's done it, I doubt it will be any more than a few quid," concluded Blake, draining the last few drops of cold coffee from his mug. "Besides, that's not my writing."

"Nor mine," said Olivia.

"Well, it's definitely not mine," confirmed Mason.

The three fell silent as they pondered the map and its possible creator.

"I doubt it was either of the police detectives," said Olivia, breaking the silence.

"Aliens," said Mason, returning to an all too familiar theme.

"It's not aliens," Blake said, sighing into his hands.

"It could be," Mason protested.

"But it isn't," Blake remained firm in his opinion. "Why would an alien doodle a map in biro?"

"It probably couldn't find a pencil," Mason explained.

"Do you recognise anywhere on the map?" Olivia asked, doing her best to steer the conversation away from little green men.

"There's a tyre swing out in the woods," Mason said. "I don't recognise anything else."

"Why don't we just go and check it out?" Olivia suggested.

"I'm going to have to get home at some point," said Blake. "I don't remember if I told my folks that I would be out all night."

"I'm in the same boat," said Olivia, "but I think we should take a look, while we're still here. I mean, none of us can remember getting drunk or anything much about yesterday at all… and then we wake up with two detectives, asleep opposite us and a map taped to the laptop. None of that sounds remotely normal and I think we should maybe try and figure out what's going on."

The boys agreed.

They left the barn, avoiding the patch of ground still covered in puke and walked into the woods, Mason taking the lead.

Aside from the terrible hangovers and general sense of confusion, it was a beautiful morning. The sun drifted through the trees, carrying the scent of leaves and blossoms and the vibrant and abundant birdsong indicated that everything was 'business as usual' as far as the wildlife was concerned.

"How far is it?" asked Blake, concerned about how awful he still felt.

"Not far, man," replied Mason, marching onwards through the woods.

"Is it your tyre swing?" asked Olivia.

"Yeah, been there since I was a kid," he reminisced. "Took my first lot of mushrooms in these woods. I remember being sat on the tyre… had Pink Floyd on the headphones. As soon as 'Any Colour You Like' kicked in, I was… whoosh… away."

"Right," said Blake, barely paying attention.

"I was gone for three days," Mason added.

"How come?"

"No idea," he shook his head as he walked, "but I think it had something to do with a hedgehog being in the way."

"You know you can just walk around those, don't you?" said Olivia.

"I do now."

"I didn't think mushrooms lasted that long?" said Blake.

"They do if you keep eating them."

"Oh."

It took another two or three minutes to reach the tyre swing and Olivia's head had started to clear a little. She could see that the boys were still struggling with their hangovers, both of them going at a sluggish pace with an occasional sigh to mark their progress.

"Well, this is it," Mason remarked, as they all came to a stop.

It was a slight clearing in the woods, with a tyre swing hanging from the thickest branch of the sturdiest looking tree.

They surveyed the area with tired eyes. They weren't sure what they would discover, but then they weren't at all sure what they were looking for.

Olivia took out the piece of paper with the crudely scribbled map on and tried to project what she saw on to her new surroundings.

"Any joy?" Blake asked, flopping himself down on to the tyre swing.

"There's the tyre swing…" she pointed to where Blake was and then looked down at the map, "and that's it. These other boxes, I would think, indicate buildings, but there aren't any."

"Has there ever been any buildings here?" Blake asked.

"I don't think so," Mason replied.

"It's showing two buildings on the map, opposite one another, just behind the tyre swing," Olivia explained.

They all thought on it for a moment, lost in the quiet of their surroundings.

"Listen, there is a good chance that it's just a scribble that doesn't mean anything," said Blake, leaning back into the tyre swing.

99

"It says 'find me'," she said.

"Well, we found the swing, didn't we?" Blake shrugged, as he began to feel pins and needles creeping into his behind.

"You alright?" Olivia asked him, noting his look of discomfort.

He didn't reply, but his eyes widened as small balls of blue light fizzed into being and drifted before him, seemingly from out of his backside.

And then he was gone.

TWENTY ONE

"All there," said Connor, having counted the grotesques.

"Thank Christ for that," said Marv, as the reverend walked around the corner to greet them. "Sorry about that, Father," he added, embarrassed by his blasphemy.

"Ah, don't be," the reverend nodded. "I thank Christ all the time. The youth of today seem so preoccupied with 'thanking fuck' for everything instead, but I don't think it would do for me to be walking around saying 'thank fuck' all the time, would it? That would be a world gone mad!"

The detectives both regarded him, blankly.

"Of course, you could argue that the world had indeed gone mad," he continued. "Plagues, poverty, persecution, that gambling octopus that kept guessing the football results…"

101

Marv frowned at that, but didn't interrupt the man. He was actually genuinely intrigued to see what would fall out of his mouth next.

"So then, nothing taken?" the vicar added.

"Nope, all good," Marv replied. "So far, at least."

"You both look shattered. Were you on stakeout all night?"

"Pretty much," lied Marv. He wasn't sure if lying to a vicar meant that you were sent to Hell, but he didn't really fancy confessing and if he was honest, he didn't believe in Hell. Or Heaven. Or much else really.

"It catches up with you," said Connor.

"Well, make sure you get some rest," said the reverend. "If you can show me how to work the cameras, you could take tonight off, if you like?"

"I don't think our boss would be very pleased if we did that," replied Connor.

"No, she's not exactly full of Christian spirit," Marv added.

"I've known a few like that," the reverend smiled. "Did you know, I once had to rugby tackle a man for stealing one of the scones from the coffee morning buffet?"

"I did not know that," Marv humoured the man.

"He actually grazed his chin quite badly. I had to give him the scone in the end. Didn't want him going to the local paper."

"Okay."

"Right, well, I'll let you both get on. I'm sure you're keen to get your heads down."

The vicar disappeared back into the chapel, leaving the detectives to walk back to the car.

"I imagine his sermons are quite lively," said Connor.

"I imagine they're quite long and winding," Marv replied.

"Definitely winding."

TWENTY TWO

Olivia looked at the empty tyre swing, dumbstruck, mouth agape, stuck for a response.

Mason was equally as stunned, but found himself walking around the tyre swing, as if to somehow prove his eyes wrong, but there was no Blake on the other side.

"Blue lights," he said, confused, perhaps unsure as to whether it was all just some extravagant flashback from a bad batch of mushrooms.

"Blue lights," Olivia repeated. "Where did he go?"

"Maybe… fae folk…"

She turned to him, bemused by her friend's unwavering belief in faeries. "Where were the faeries, Mason?"

"Well… I…"

"There weren't any. There's no such thing as sodding faeries!"

He paused for a moment, a little hurt at Olivia's outburst.

"Aliens?" he offered.

"How long has your tyre swing been magic?" she asked, ignoring his comment altogether.

"It never did that when I used to sit on it," he replied. "Maybe Blake's got a magic arse."

"Wait, is this some kind of trick?" she asked. "Because, normally that would be very clever, but today..."

"If it is, it's nothing to do with me!" Mason protested, holding his hands up.

"Well, I don't think Blake would have the energy or focus to come up with something like this on his own," she reasoned.

"I think we need to sit on the tyre," Mason said, although every syllable seemed to fall out of his mouth awkwardly and without conviction.

"Is that really a good idea?" she asked, taking a few deep breaths to cure her of the light-headedness threatening to swamp her. "We don't know where... or what..."

"We can't just leave him... wherever he is."

"Maybe he'll be back in a minute."

"Maybe."

"We should probably just give him a minute or two."

"Okay."

They remained stood, though Olivia could quite easily have fallen on the ground and hyperventilated. She still couldn't believe what was happening, although she had no idea of what was actually happening at all.

They remained there, in the clearing, looking at the tyre swing in silence.

After what felt like two minutes, Mason coughed to clear his throat.

"He's not back," he said, stating the obvious.

She took a deep breath, filling her lungs with courage, before walking over to the tyre and sitting on it.

"You feel okay?" Mason asked.

"I haven't felt okay all morn…" And then she felt the tingling in her posterior. "…I think something is happening."

A second or two later and the same small blue lights that had emanated from behind Blake began to appear from behind Olivia and a shimmer of light later and she too was gone.

"Aliens," Mason said, walking over to the tyre, sitting down and closing his eyes.

*

Olivia felt the blue fizz sweep through her body and then she fell on to the ground in front of the tyre swing.

It took her a moment to gain her composure. She sat up and held her hands out in front of her, checking to see if they looked like they were fizzing. They felt very much like they were fizzing. They weren't fizzing, thankfully.

She looked up to the clearing in the woods, except that it wasn't a clearing in the woods anymore. The tyre swing was behind her, hanging from a single tree, rooted to a patch of grass around ten feet long and six wide. Either side of the patch were two large buildings, around thirty feet away. She assumed they were buildings... they were actually nothing more than gigantic concrete rectangles with no windows, some fifty feet high.

Between the buildings, running in a long line stretching as far as she could see, was patch after patch, each with something slightly different in it. The next one along had a burnt out Ford Capri in it, with its boot open and the one after that, a rusted iron door between two stone pillars. They went on, thirty, forty or even fifty, perhaps, until the small scenes became too small to make out in the distance.

Mason landed on her.

They both collapsed in a heap.

"Jesus..." she mumbled from under his legs.

He jumped up, too quickly, only to fall again, like a newly born foal finding its legs.

"What the...?"

"It's alright," she said, trying to calm him down, as he sat upright and stared at his hands. "They're not fizzing," she added.

"They're fizzing," he announced, panicked at the sensation.

"They just feel like it. It wears off," she assured him.

He took control of his breathing, taking in deep breaths and releasing them slowly as he surveyed the scene before him.

"Where are we?" he asked.

"I've no idea. I'd be very surprised if it was Chapel-on-the-Moss though."

They both looked out now, taking in the litter of other scenes stretching out before them, flanked as they were by the tall concrete structures.

The sky was a dirty yellow, and yet they weren't sure if it was day or night. It still seemed quite dark everywhere, as if the sky had very little to do with their surroundings at all.

106

Their eyes strayed to the buildings, both sporting unfurled black banners running almost their full height, at the top of which sat a red triangle with a white top.

"Factories?" Mason said, trying to fathom what he was seeing.

"Psst!"

They looked around for what had made the noise.

"Psst. Over here!"

"Blake?" Olivia called, eventually noticing him peeking from behind the dilapidated Ford Capri.

She scurried over to him, urging Mason to do the same. He did so, still in a daze, keeping low to the ground.

"Are you alright?" Olivia asked as she reached Blake, squatting low at the side of the car.

"Are you?" he asked.

"It's probably a bit early to say."

"Where are we, man?" asked Mason.

"I literally just got here a minute before you did," Blake shrugged.

"Wherever it is, it looks pretty shady. I think we should just go straight back," Olivia suggested.

"That was the first thing I tried, but it doesn't seem to work," said Blake.

"I'll try it again," said Mason, shuffling off over to the patch of grass with the tyre swing. He climbed back through the tyre, but simply fell out on the other side.

"Shit," said Olivia, as Mason quickly re-joined them at the car.

"Have you still got the map?" Blake asked.

Olivia pulled the crumpled piece of paper from out of her pocket, unfolded it and handed it to Blake.

"Those squares are the two buildings," he said, pointing from the map to the huge concrete structures looming large before them. "There's this dotted line going towards the building on the left." He pointed back to the map. "There's a smaller square in the bottom left corner of the large square."

"And?" Olivia asked.

"And maybe we should check it out?"

"Wait a minute. You want to go in there?" Olivia seemed appalled at the idea.

"I don't 'want' to go in there, but I'm not sure what other options we have right now."

"One option is not going in there…" it was her turn to point at the building, "…in the large, scary-looking building with no windows."

"We already tried going back," said Blake. "I'm not sure what else there is to do?"

She was a little stumped at that. Every fibre of her being dictated that this was a 'run away' situation. Snake? Run away. Serial killer? Run away. Large foreboding concrete building next to a magic tyre swing? Run away.

"I've just seen enough films in my time to know when walking into something is a bad idea!" she explained.

"Well, maybe you should stay here and Mason and I could go and check out the building?" Blake suggested.

"Split up?" she scoffed. "That's literally the other stupid thing people do in films!"

Mason reached into his back pocket and pulled out half a joint, crooked and extremely worse for wear.

"Really… that's your idea? That's your contribution to getting out of here?" Olivia asked.

"Just a thought," he replied, placing it carefully back in the pocket.

The siren stunned the three of them into petrified silence. It echoed between the two buildings and then they noticed three figures leaving the building to their left, through a small door, heading towards the patches.

TWENTY THREE

They had knocked on the door of the barn and waited, before knocking again and having a nose around the crumbling building. Marv had spotted the area of sick that they had contributed to earlier that morning and had replayed the ordeal in his mind.

They had then wandered out into the woods, searching for anything that might have caused the lights from the night before.

"Anything?" Marv asked, having wandered in the opposite direction to his partner.

"An old toilet seat," he replied, nudging it with his foot as it rested in a clump of tall grass by a tree.

"Not something I would bring to a picnic, but then it takes all sorts, I suppose."

"It does make you wonder why someone would bring something like that out here," Connor said, moving away from the item and closer to Marv again.

"I'm thinking maybe the stoner thought it would be funny," said Marv.

"You seem to think stoners find anything funny."

"Look, it's on the stoner's property, ergo it probably belongs to the stoner," Marv reasoned.

"Circumstantial," Connor argued.

"Irrelevant," Marv pointed out. "It's a toilet seat and has nothing to do with what we're looking for anyway."

"Fair enough," the younger man agreed. "It's difficult to know what we are looking for really."

"Anything that's not a tree or a toilet seat has potential."

They continued their search, happening upon a rusting scooter being reclaimed by the undergrowth, an old tyre swing and a broken wooden stool. As far as searches went, it hadn't been particularly fruitful.

"We're not really getting anywhere. I think we should probably head back to the office and report in," said Marv, enthusiasm distinctly lacking in his voice.

His partner agreed and they slowly made their way back to the car.

*

The office seemed a little busier than usual; the bustle a little bustlier, the officers a little more focused in their actions.

"I think we missed something," said Connor, as Sergeant Cole walked out of her office.

111

"Ah, step this way, gentlemen," she said, and for once there was no name calling tacked on to the sentence.

"No grotesques stolen last night," Marv began, trying to sound less tired than he was.

"Forget about the church for now," she interrupted. "We have more pressing things to think about."

Both Marv and Connor liked the sound of that, something that might actually resemble police work as opposed to baby-sitting statues.

"Really?" Marv asked, eyebrows high with expectation.

"We had a missing person reported this morning. She didn't come home last night, which is apparently out of character, but her parents figured she was probably just staying over with friends. They called everybody they can think of, but nobody has seen her."

"Right," Marv said, with a genuine zeal and vitality he hadn't had since his first weeks in the job.

"I've not finished," she interrupted his keenness. "In calling her friends, the mother discovered that one of her male friends also failed to come home last night, so now we're potentially looking for two missing people."

"Okay," said Marv, enthused as perhaps never before. "How old are they?"

"Both nineteen," she replied.

"Young lovers eloping, perhaps?" Marv suggested.

"That might have made sense if the parents disapproved of the friendship, but they liked the guy and by all accounts, they were just friends anyway."

Both detectives sat quietly, mulling over the possible reasons for such a disappearance. The area wasn't exactly known for its nefarious criminal exploits and so the most likely cause was

112

going to be something much more mundane than kidnapping or foul play.

"We have officers out with the families now and some out making enquiries in town. I thought you two would be best over in Chapel-on-the-Moss, since you've been out that way recently."

"Okay," they both agreed, though being ordered back to the village had knocked a little of the wind from their sails.
"All the information is on your desk, along with some recent photos. I know you've both pulled an all-nighter, but if you've got something left in the tank, I'd appreciate you working a few hours over."

"No problem," they said in unison.

They left the office, both feeling something close to being back in the boss's good books and that was a feeling long since forgotten.

"I know I shouldn't say this, because people are missing, but I'll just be glad that we're not sat staring at a graveyard," Marv said, walking over to his desk and picking up the print-out.

"Yeah. Cole even seemed quite happy to see us," said Connor.

"Enjoy it while it lasts," Marv replied, staring disconcertingly at the photos of Olivia Gatley and Blake Norton.

TWENTY FOUR

The three men hadn't ventured too close to their location, but they had hidden behind the car and remained extremely quiet in any case, not wanting be discovered.

Mason had chanced a peek, as the men had come to a plot, some five or six plots away from them. They had stopped at what looked like an entrance to a cave. One of the men had wiped some sort of card against the rock and then they had disappeared within a multitude of small blue lights.

They had looked familiar to him, those men. Tall, well-built, shaven heads, dressed in black.

"What is it?" Blake asked. "Are they gone?"

"Yeah," Mason said, returning his attention to his friends by the car. "I think I've seen those men before."

"Someone you know?" Olivia asked.

"No. I don't think I know them, but I'm sure I've seen them somewhere." He closed his eyes, squeezing them tightly as if that would aid his memory. "Maybe it's déjà vu."

"Look, I think we need to go and get some answers here," said Blake.

"I agree," Olivia said, grudgingly.

"Really?" Blake looked surprised. "I was expecting to have to convince you."

"Well, I suppose we can't just sit here forever, can we?" she replied. "As much as it pains me to say it, I don't think we have any other choice but to check out the building. That's what it says on the map and right now we don't know how to get back home and so we need to find out."

"Okay then," both Blake and Mason agreed.

"That being said, the building still looks extremely scary and so let's all agree not to split up."

They moved warily, treading carefully between the lengthy line of small scenes, before eventually veering off, over a gravel path and down towards the side of the building and to the door they had seen the men leave through.

"Why is the sky yellow?" Mason mumbled to nobody in particular as he went.

"Why is there a magic tyre? Why are there loads of different small plots of land in a line? Why can't we remember last night? The list goes on!" said Olivia.

They reached the side of the building and squatted to the right of the black door, scanning their immediate surroundings to make sure they hadn't been seen.

"I suppose we just go in then?" said Blake, looking at the others.

"Unless you were thinking of ringing the doorbell?" Olivia teased.

He tried the handle and sure enough the door clicked open. Part of him had hoped it was going to be locked. He tried his best to ignore that part of himself as he looked in through the doorway.

There were a few concrete steps going down, leading to a long, dimly lit concrete corridor, but that was as much as he could see from his position outside the building.

"Just a corridor," he said to the others.

"Are we going in?" asked Mason.

"I suppose so. I mean, it looks safe."

"Okay. Lead the way," Olivia said.

"You want me to go first?" Blake asked, as casually as he could, worried, but doing his best to hide it.

"With your considerable Call Of Duty experience, I think it's best if we followed you in."

"Right. I'm not entirely sure that's relevant to this situation…" he muttered, allowing the sentence to fade into nothingness.

"Your reflexes…" Olivia tried to add to the range of skills, but found it difficult because she knew she was talking complete rubbish. "You'll be sharp… ready for trouble."

Blake stepped through the doorway and down the steps. Olivia followed closely behind and Mason brought up the rear, pulling the door to, but not clicking it shut, just in case they needed to beat a hasty retreat.

It was a long corridor. There also didn't seem to be any doors leading off it and so they ambled along in single-file, their senses on alert, eyes focused on the end of the corridor, which, as they neared it, formed a T junction.

116

There was a sign on the wall directly in front of them, at the top of which was an arrow pointing left and then the words…

CATALOGUING
ALPHA SECTION
ATTACHMENT

And then an arrow pointing right and the words…

AGENT STATION
OMEGA ROOMS
WASTE

"Well, I'm not sure we're looking for any of those," said Blake.

"What exactly are we looking for?" asked Mason.

They all stood for a moment of quiet to ponder the complexities of the situation.

"That's actually a good question," said Olivia.

"Answers," said Blake, taking another look at the sign, "but 'answers' isn't on there." He honestly hadn't expected it to be, but he was rather hoping to find something a little less cryptic than the options on display. In truth, he wasn't sure that he really wanted to bump into anybody in this strange place, but other than stumbling across a book with all the answers in it, called 'Answers', it was a likely eventuality that he would, at some point have to ask someone what the Hell was going on.

"Shall we just randomly pick a department to head for?" Olivia asked.

"Let's go to Waste," said Mason.

"I don't think it means 'get wasted'," Olivia said, trying to inform his decision making.

"I know. It has generally been my experience in life," he said, as if he had lived a good many more years than he actually had, "that the people who do jobs requiring a bit more graft are usually a bit more down to earth. Hopefully they'll be more likely to help us out?"

"Okay. As far as theories go, it's not terrible," agreed Blake.

"It's also the only theory we have," Olivia added.

"Right it is then," Blake said and led them down the right-hand corridor.

This corridor was as long as the last, but had wooden doors on either side; Agent Station 1, 2 and 3 on the left and Omega Room 1, 2 and 3 on the right. The door marked 'Waste' was at the end of the corridor and Blake took a deep breath before opening and peering in through the doorway.

It was a large room filled with the noise of mechanical equipment and pumps; a backdrop to their nervousness. The whole place was a labyrinth of pipes and gauges, dials and steam vents, all seemingly thrown around the place with little care or planning, although Blake was sure there was a logic to the design, at least in the eyes of those that designed it.

"What kind of waste do we think is in here?" asked Olivia, as she too stepped into the room, followed by Mason, who seemed impressed at the scale of clutter.

"Alien waste," he said. "Maybe it's Area 51?"

"I really don't think we're in Nevada," said Blake, although he didn't have much of a clue where they were.

"Well, we're *definitely* not in Chapel-on-the-Moss."

"Can I help yer?" said the man, that they hadn't seen, stood right next to them.

It made the three of them jump a little and did nothing to settle their nerves.

He wore the decaying carcass of an ancient black baseball cap

118

and a set of dirty brown overalls, dotted with the same triangular insignia from the unfurled banners on the outside of the buildings and a nametag declaring him to be called Wink. His shortage of teeth, as he stood open-mouthed, oil-stained hands and long, unkempt beard with knots of food and tobacco tangled within led them to believe the man wasn't exactly high on the executive ladder. Much of the oil on his face had sunken into the deep lines and served only to highlight his advancing years.

"Sorry, yes…. erm, Wink, is it?" asked Blake, politely, noting the name and trying to build a friendly connection to the best of his ability and despite himself.

"Yeah."

"That's an unusual name."

"My real name's Endoligent Winkfell-Brayzmikkeland. People call me Wink for short," he replied, in a thick east-end accent.

"I bet they do," said Olivia.

"Erm… is this 'Waste'?" Blake asked, trying to appear lost, though he had never truly felt more lost than he was right now.

"Says so on the door, donit?"

"It does," Blake agreed fretfully. "Always best to check though. Listen, we are a bit lost and I wondered if you could help us out?"

"New, are yer?"

"Something like that."

"Alright, well, where dya wanna be?"

It was a straight-forward sort of question, but Blake didn't have a straight-forward sort of answer.

"I don't really know," he eventually replied.

"I reckon we might struggle to get yer there then," came the rather obvious reply.

119

"Actually," Blake said, pulling the map from his pocket and unravelling it, "I suppose we could do with going here?"

Blake handed the creased piece of paper over and Wink took it, smudging the edges with his oil-stained fingers.

"Looks like Alpha Section to me," he said, noting the crudely scribbled words 'find me' on the paper, as he handed it back.

"Alpha Section?" Blake asked.

Wink nodded. "Something tells me that you aint too familiar with the place?" It might have sounded like a question, but it was a statement.

"Did us being lost swing that for you?" Olivia mumbled to herself.

"I'm not sure what you'd want over in Alpha Section," Wink continued. "You don't much strike me as portal personnel."

"I'll be honest," Blake said, tentatively. "We're sort of here by accident."

"Okay," Wink replied, seemingly unphased by the admission.

"And we're not really sure of where 'here' is."

"Bloody Bleachers left a door open again, didn't they?"

The three of them shrugged, although Blake recognised the word from somewhere, but it was a memory that remained frustratingly just out of reach.

"Well, here is Zenith, but that probably won't mean much to yer."

The name rang a bell with all three of them and they all stood silent for a few seconds, their brains going into overdrive to find information on it.

"I do know that name," said Blake, "and I've heard of Bleachers too, but I can't really remember..."

"Well, it sounds like the Bleachers did a number on yer, injected yer with the Wipe Serum."

They stared blankly back at him.

"Most won't remember a thing, takes a day or so from yer. Some are lucky, get snippets come back to 'em, but you'll have felt sick as a dog when yer came to."

They all remembered that part, vividly. Blake instinctively wiped his hand over his ear, recalling the hot vomit from earlier. He tried not to think about it.

"So we were drugged?" Olivia said, anger in her voice.

"Expect so," Wink nodded.

"Why?" she asked.

"Well, folks over there aint really supposed to know about us folks over here."

"Where is here, exactly?" Blake asked.

"Is it Area 51?" Mason quickly added.

"It's Zenith," Wink said. "Told yer that already."

"Is the place called Zenith or is the company that owns the factory called Zenith?" Olivia asked.

Wink thought for a moment, looking a little baffled at the question. "It's the same thing," he eventually replied. "The place is the factory and the factory is the place."

Blake rubbed a hand over his face, struggling to grasp the nub of the response.

"Are you aliens?" Mason asked, although by now even he was beginning to doubt the possibility.

"Listen, I get that yer all outta sorts, but truth be told, yer got yerselves a problem here. If yer came through by accident, ten-to-one yer can't get yerselves back."

"We tried to go back through…" Blake confirmed.

"Yep, yer need a card to change the polarity."

"Oh. Do you have one?" he asked, as hopeful as he dared to be.

121

"Son, this is 'Waste'."

"No card?"

Wink shook his head. "Unless I was planning to offload the waste over to the other side, which I have thought about, they wouldn't give me a card. I have no business outside of my department."

"Do you know where we could get a card?" Again, hope reigned supreme in Blake's voice.

"I'd imagine Alpha Section would be a good bet, but I don't imagine you'd get in or outta there without some trouble. I'm real surprised that yer got yerselves this far without being stopped."

The three of them looked at the worker with puppy dog eyes.

"Any chance you might be able to give us a hand with that?" asked Blake.

TWENTY FIVE

"So, we're not telling Cole that we saw them?" said Connor, keeping his eyes on the road, as they made their way to the 'stoner's barn'.

"You actually think we should?" Marv said, his eyes wide in surprise.

"I wouldn't go that far," he backtracked. "Let's just say I'm on the fence."

"I don't want to make any snap-decisions, that's all," Marv explained. "Cole might have a few questions like 'what were you doing at the barn?' and 'why weren't you watching the church?' and 'what do you mean you can't remember?' I just think it might be better to sit on the information whilst we have time to take a look around the place and ask some questions."

123

"Well, there was nobody there this morning," said Connor.

"Thanks for that. Are you going to just sit there and state the obvious all day? That would be really helpful."

"I'm just saying!"

"Well, maybe they've come back by now and if not, we can ask around, maybe do a spot of actual detective work. If nothing presents itself, then we go to Cole. Just remember though, it's going to be a little bit difficult for us to explain why we were there when we don't actually know."

"That's true," Connor agreed with his partner.

"In any case, I'm not sure 'mysterious flashing lights' is going to be a story she will want to hear. Can you remember having to explain how we ended up locked in the toilets of that restaurant whilst we were looking for those missing pigeons?"

"I can," Connor confirmed.

"Now throw in some missing people and some UFOs and imagine how that conversation might go."

They pulled off the road and parked up near to the barn, as they had done earlier that day.

As they exited the car, they both had a good look at the scenery, the trees, the dry-stone walls, the old metal gates and Marv noticed a farmhouse further up the tree-lined dirt track.

Connor knocked on the door, four hard raps so that they couldn't go unheard.

"I'll check round the back," Marv said, walking to the right of the barn and following it as far as he could go. It was all waist-high weeds and nettles round the back and so he returned to the front of the building as Connor gave several more loud knocks on the door.

"I think we should go up to the farm," Marv suggested.

Connor agreed and they strolled up the dirt track, taking in the fields and woodland as they went, enjoying the sun as it appeared and disappeared behind banks of meandering clouds.

They approached the farmhouse and walked by the red tractor parked outside. This building looked in a much better state than the barn, despite its obvious years.

Connor knocked on the wooden door and heard the dog bark from inside. He hoped it was well behaved or confined to another part of the house. He wasn't keen on dogs, ever since his friend's rottweiler had latched on to the bottom of his trousers in his youth. It had refused to let go for the best part of an hour. His friend had promised that the dog would get bored before he did, but boredom hadn't been the overriding emotion that had gripped him.

A pleasant woman in her late forties opened the door and greeted them. From the smell that wafted through from inside, they guessed that she was in the middle of baking.

"Hello?" she asked, wiping a strand of hair from her face and smearing flour on to her cheek in the process.

"Hi, I'm Detective Weaving and this is my partner, Detective Raines," said Marv. "We're sorry to disturb you, but would you mind if we asked you a few questions about the occupant of the barn at the bottom of your track?"

"My son, Mason?" she replied.

"Mason, yes. He's your son?" Marv said, motioning to Connor to write it down.

"Yes. What's he in trouble for now? Has he been smoking cannibals again?" she asked.

"Cannabis," Connor corrected her.

"I've told him until I'm blue in the face about all that nonsense, but you know what boys of that age are like. I keep out of it now, and I suppose it could be worse. At least he's not doing any of that crackling or smash."

125

"I was wondering if you knew where he was at the minute?" Marv asked. "He's not in any trouble. We just want to ask him a few questions about something."

"I thought he was in," she said, shrugging her shoulders a little. "He must have had some friends round last night. I think they must have had a party in the woods over there, because I saw the lights through the trees. At least they kept the music down though, we didn't hear a peep."

"Right, but you haven't seen him this morning?"

"No, but then I wouldn't expect to really. He's not what you'd call an early riser at the best of times, but after a party…" she trailed off. "Probably won't see him for a few days, until he needs some washing doing."

"Do you have any idea where he might have gone, a friend's perhaps or somewhere he likes to hang out?"

"He's friends with Blake - Blake Norton, has been since school. He always seemed like a nice enough boy."

"Okay," Marv dug a little further. "Nobody else?"

"Sometimes there's a girl with them… erm, Liv, I think they call her. You sure he's not in any trouble?" she added.

"He's not," Marv assured her. "We're just asking around as Blake Norton and Olivia Gatley didn't return home last night."

"Oh dear," she said, concern in her eyes.

"More than likely, they've stayed over at a friend's house or at a party," Marv was quick to say, "but here's my card," he added, handing it over. "If you hear from Mason, would you just let me know so that I might ask him a few questions?"

"I will," she replied.

"I'm sure they're fine," he reiterated. "You know what that age group is like," he reminded her.

TWENTY SIX

They had waited for over half an hour in a darkened corner of the large and noisy waste room, among the pipes and behind some looming iron vats.

Wink had told them to 'keep out of the way' and so they sat tight and waited.

"Is anyone else about to have a panic attack?" asked Blake, looking paler and more worried than he had probably ever looked.

"We're going to be alright," Olivia said, in an unconvincing attempt to calm him.

"Are we? Are you basing that on the fact that we don't know where we are or what's going on?"

"I was lying," she admitted. "There's actually a good chance that 'Mr Hygiene' is ratting us out and we're all about to be shot."

"Oh," Blake reeled. "Go back to lying."

"Let's just think about this logically," Mason said.

They looked at him, eyebrows raised, awaiting some surprising nugget of reason, but expecting some half-baked theory about aliens or goblins.

"There's a lot of weird stuff going on…" he began.

"I think you're going to need to do a lot better than that," Olivia interrupted.

"Let's catalogue the weird stuff…"

"Okay, well, we're in some sort of ominous factory in a weird place that has yellow sky and we got here by sitting on a magic tyre swing." She was quite happy with her summing up of the situation, but it hadn't exactly helped her join any dots.

"We all woke up with a hangover, but none of us remember drinking," said Blake.

"We don't remember anything really from the day before, so it's safe to assume that Wink was maybe right about the… was it, Bleachers?"

Blake and Olivia both nodded. "Yeah, Bleachers."

"And I seemed to remember the tall, bald guys we saw outside… maybe they're Bleachers?"

"Okay," said Blake. "But why drug us to make us forget something when we don't know anything to begin with?"

"But we don't know that we don't know anything, because they drugged us to make us forget what we know, so we still might know it."

It didn't sound like it should have made sense, but it sort of did.

"It's obviously something to do with who made the map," said Blake. "Before we found the map, we all got the feeling that someone was missing, right?"

Thinking was beginning to hurt, but they continued as best as they could.

"We went to Irene's Kettle," said Olivia, racking her brains. "Was anybody else there?"

"I doubt it," Blake scoffed. "There's only us that don't seem to mind cold tea."

They heard the door go, some fifteen to twenty feet away from them and they froze, hoping that it was Wink.

"Just me!" Wink called out, walking towards them.

They stood from behind the vats, their relief written large upon their faces.

"Any luck?" Olivia asked.

"No," came the rather abrupt reply.

"Oh," said Blake.

"I think I know where the cards are kept though," he continued.

"Oh," said Blake, with a little more optimism in his voice.

"But I can't get 'em for yer," he added.

"Oh," said Blake, once again deflated.

"I sympathise with yer predicament n' all, but if I got caught taking one o' those cards, that'd be me for the chop, yer understand?"

"We do," said Olivia. "Thanks for trying anyway."

"I *can* show yer where they are," he said, still wanting to help to some degree.

"How would we get there?" Blake asked.

"I have a spare uniform in the back yer can borrow and I can point yer in the right direction," he offered.

"Okay," Blake thought about it. "Just one uniform?"

"Yeah, one of yer would have to go get a card and then come back for the others."

They all looked at each other.

"That sounds like fun," said Blake.

"It really doesn't," Olivia remarked.

"I'll give it a go," said Mason.

"Really?" asked Blake.

"Listen, not to put too finer point on it, but the pair of you might look a bit too clean to be 'waste' employees," Mason explained. "I however, still have beans in my beard."

"I did notice the beans," agreed Wink.

"Are you sure?" Olivia asked.

"I think so. I can be pretty covert when I need to be."

"The uniform is in the office at the back there," Wink pointed to show Mason the way. "Yer should have about an hour to get this done. We're on a down shift at the minute, so there's just me in here, but there'll be another eight people in soon to get the pumps going."

"Just in case you wanted some extra pressure," added Blake.

TWENTY SEVEN

Mason strolled down the corridor towards Alpha Section, nervous, but looking every bit the Waste employee in his oil-stained uniform. He was humming some random tune that may have started out as an actual tune, but had quickly descended into a meandering noise.

He reached the signed junction from earlier and continued on until he reached a door marked 'Alpha Section', where he took a deep breath before entering into another long corridor with numerous doors leading off from both sides.

He looked at the palm of his left hand, where he had written the door number he needed... AS5.

As he looked up, two men, both dressed in grey uniform, exited from a door just ahead and to Mason's left.

They both looked him up and down.

131

"You forget where 'Waste' is, son?" asked the older and larger of the two.

"Literally just came from there," said Mason, trying to remain relaxed.

"And why are you down this way?" the same man asked.

"Wink said he had a report of, erm…" he struggled to think of something, "… a damaged spool shaft… valve."

"Really?"

"Yeah, bloody spool shaft valves, man."

"Right," said the man, both he and his partner looking mildly perplexed.

"They're everywhere in this place, but most of them are only…" he coughed a little to clear the dryness in his throat, "…partially truncated so they just… flex out." Even he knew he was rambling.

"Where you headed?"

"AS5," he replied.

The men stepped out of his way and then went on with their business.

Mason tried to let his sigh of relief out slowly so that the men wouldn't hear it, but it was a huge sigh. He wasn't sure if he had actually breathed at all whilst talking to them.

He reached AS5 and walked through the door.

It was an office very much like other offices. People were in typical office-wear, head down in their ledgers and monitors, at least until he walked in and then all eyes were on him.

"Erm… hi?" he said, quietly. "Don't let me disturb you. I'm just here to check on the spool shaft valve."

The faces that met his gaze were as oblivious as he had hoped they would be.

As the people steadily returned their attention to their work again, Mason allowed his eyes to scan the desks and trays for any 'polarity cards' whilst moving around the wall, knocking and pretending to listen for any 'flexing' on the 'valves'.

He spotted a card that looked exactly as Wink had described, red with a black strip and three blue circles on the edge. It was on top of a stack of paperwork in a tray on the desk of the bitter-looking woman, now staring back at him.

He knocked on the wall again.

"That's it," he said. "That's so flexed."

She continued her unmoving gaze.

"Don't worry, this won't take long," he assured her. "The spool shaft valve behind this wall is flexed. It happens all the time. It's because they didn't truncate the…"

"Why are you telling me this?" she asked, agitated, annoyed at his being there.

"Oh… okay, I'll be…" he stuttered to a silence, before wondering exactly how he would take the card or indeed, fix the so called problem behind the wall.

"Actually," he began, "I'll show you a cool trick and it will save me going back for my tools."

She let out a deep huff of air and looked up at him again, unimpressed with his continued harassment.

He took the card from out of her work tray and tapped it against the wall a few times, before moving it down the wall and doing the same again.

"This usually works… the polarity destabilises the flexing… circumnavigates the erm…" He pretended to look confused, before knocking on the wall a few more times and listening in. "That's strange. This card doesn't seem to be working."

"You're right. That was a cool trick, thanks," she said before turning her eyes back to her screen.

"I just need to check the… stabiliser…" he waffled. "I'll be back in about ten to fifteen…"

133

He walked out of the office in faux annoyance at having to do 'more work' and back out into the corridor, the card in his pocket, a smile creeping on to his face. The other men were no longer in the corridor and so he strolled along, relishing the win and feeling rather pleased with himself.

As he walked along he glanced at the doors to his right, AS4 down to AS1. The last door had a sign next to it that simply read 'Holding'. There was a small rectangular window on the door and he could see a man in there; a rather familiar looking man who rushed to the door upon seeing him looking in.

"You!" said Ven, both shocked and elated to see a familiar face peering back at him.

Mason's eyes narrowed, his brain struggling to place the face and eventually coming up empty-handed.

"I'm sorry, man," he replied. "I can't remember you. Don't take that personally though, I'm pretty sure it's because of drugs."

"It's me, Ven!" he said.

Mason shook his head. "Sorry. Kind of recognise you, but..."

"I was at your barn. You took me in because I was in danger. We ate mashed potatoes and beans..." Ven continued to list things in a hope to jogging his memory.

"I do eat that a lot," Mason agreed.

"Your name is..." he thought hard and then it came to him, "Mason!"

"Well, I can remember that."

"You obviously found the map!"

"Wait. You drew the map?"

"Yes!" he cried, finally getting somewhere. "Listen, you need to get me out of this room and I'll get us out of here!"

"Could you tell us what the hell is going on too?" he asked.

"I'll tell you everything."

THE KNOWING

TWENTY EIGHT

Marv and Connor sat down at the table by the window and looked out to the street beyond, just as the sun disappeared behind the clouds.

"Supposed to rain later," Connor said, trying to wipe the tired from his eyes.

Marv didn't respond but picked up the small menu and gazed at the handful of options.

"I'm starving," he eventually said.

A moment later and Irene shuffled out of the kitchen and over to the table.

"Good afternoon," she said in her sweet but fragile voice.

Marv looked a little amazed that the woman was still able to stand, but replied with his order anyway.

"Hello. Could I have a coffee and a cheese toastie, please?"

"I'll have the same," said Connor.

"Okay," she said, before slowly walking back into the kitchen.

"I feel as tired as she looks," said Marv, once she was back in the kitchen.

"Well, this should help keep us going for a few hours."

"Yeah. We'll give it another hour or two and then head home to get our heads down until tonight."

Connor appeared lost in thought. "I'm just wondering, if they are still in the area, where is there to actually go? It's not exactly the most stimulating of places."

"We should check the park," said Marv, "but that will take all of two minutes, it's tiny. There are some trees to the side of it and some allotments too."

"I suppose there's the river walk?" Connor suggested.

"I reckon they'll have more luck investigating in town," said Marv. "They'll probably be in the student pub, drinking away the hangover."

"That actually sounds like a decent idea," Connor smiled. "Although I think I've got to the age where I'd take sleep over drinking."

"I've got to the age where I'd take sleep over being awake," Marv smiled.

The food arrived after around ten minutes. Two omelettes and two cans of coke. Marv was about to say something, but the omelettes looked and smelled divine and so they both just tucked in.

"Actually, I don't suppose you've seen either of these people?" Marv asked, through a mouthful of egg, taking the pictures from his pocket and showing them to the old lady.

She scrutinised the pictures with a steely squint.

137

"Yes," she replied, before turning to leave for the kitchen.

"Erm… could I ask where you saw them?" Marv added, a little bemused.

"On your photo, my dear," she said, turning back to them, slowly.

"Right." Marv gave his partner a wide-eyed look and Connor smiled. "Thank you, that was very helpful."

"They were in here yesterday," she continued, "with the man from the bin."

"Oh," said Marv, his interest peaked.

"The man from the bin?" asked Connor.

TWENTY NINE

"So, what exactly is this place?" asked Olivia, keen to fill the time waiting for Mason with answers. "What does it do?"

"Well, not to put too fine a point on it, it's sposed to be a secret," Wink replied. "Folks on your side aint sposed to know about it."

"But we're here, so we already know about it," said Blake.

"Yer got me there," he shrugged.

"What do you mean by our side?" Olivia asked.

"Well now, I don't know where your science is currently up to. I heard some great things, but by all accounts you got yourselves a way to go yet." He paused for a moment, to chew over how best to explain.

"I think we'll be able to understand," Olivia assured him.

"Alright, well, the universe aint as black and white as you think. For a start, there's a shit load more of it than you know."

"Okay," she said, nodding to assure him that she was following him, so far.

"Space is filled with more spaces. The universe looks flat as hell, but you're just seeing one layer. If you imagine space as a coat, try and imagine it as a coat with a lot of pockets, inside and outside."

"So this is a pocket?" Blake asked.

"Yeah,"

"And so our side is the coat?"

"Nope. Your side is just another pocket. Pockets everywhere. The whole universe is just made up of pockets."

"And the tyre?" he asked.

"'Scuse me?"

"We came through a tyre…"

"Ah, those are the portals… just a bunch o' different portals to your pocket."

"Just our pocket?" Olivia asked.

"It's the only pocket we can get to."

A blast of steam erupted from a vent, high up in the room, startling them for a moment. Wink picked up a spanner from a toolbox on the floor and climbed a ladder to the left of the vent. Within a minute he had fixed the issue and re-joined the discussion.

"Where were we up to?" Wink asked.

"Pockets," said Blake and Olivia, in unison.

"Right, whole universe is full of 'em."

"But how do you know that, if you can only get to our pocket?" Olivia asked.

"Well, if you believe the stories, and I got no reason not to,

140

our founder comes from one... another one, I mean... one that aint this pocket or the one you're from."

"And who's your founder?" asked Blake, his mouth hanging open slightly, hanging on Wink's answers.

"Vitmyre," Wink replied. "Old as Hell and twice as senile. Still, he keeps this place running, so I guess he aint got both feet over the rainbow just yet."

"His name doesn't ring a bell," said Blake.

"No reason why it should."

"And so, do you guard the portals here?" asked Olivia.

"We make 'em," Wink replied.

"Why?"

"To come over to your side," Wink stated, bluntly, as if she wasn't quite getting the gist of what he was saying.

"I mean, why are you coming over to our side?" she elaborated.

"Course correction."

"That rings a bell," said Blake as the main door opened and Mason hurried through.

"Did you get a card?" Olivia asked.

"Yeah, but there's something else." They waited, uneasy and hanging on his words. "Does anybody remember a guy called Ven?"

Both Blake and Olivia shook their head, but the name registered with Wink.

"I do," he said. "We go way back. He defected a few days back. Do you know him?" Wink asked Mason.

"No. Well, yeah. I think so." He walked towards them and handed Olivia the card. "He's the one that drew the map."

"So it's his fault we're here?" she said, a little sourly.

"They've got him locked in a room. He says he'll get us back home if we get him out of there."

141

"We have the card," said Olivia, holding it up.

"Yeah, we can already get back," said Blake.

"He seemed straight up, man. I think we know him and that's why our memories got wiped."

They all looked at Wink.

"Wait a minute, now. I like the guy but showing you guys where to get a card to get home is a hell of a difference to springing a defected agent. That would land me in some serious shit; liable to get me erased."

Wink let out a huge sigh, feeling the weight of expectation from the newcomers, as well as a tug of conscience. He had known Ven for some years and classed him as a friend, a good man too, which was rare enough. It didn't seem right that a good man be locked away for trying to get out.

"Well, the cell door will, more than likely have a magnetised bolt, so a magnetic relay should do the trick. I should have one in the back."

"Thank you, Wink," said Blake. "You've been..."

Wink waved away the compliment and disappeared off into a side room to grab whatever tool would help them.

"You sure about this?" Olivia asked Mason.

"Seems like the right thing to do."

THIRTY

The three of them had left the waste department, and
traversed the same corridors that Mason had, just moments
prior. As before, Wink had kept out of it, handing over the
magnetic relay device and explaining how to use it, before
wishing them luck.

"Best if yer don't head back this way," he had said. "The
others are due on shift soon and some of them have a little
more career ambition than I do."

They had thanked him for all his help. He had, after all, done
more than they could have hoped for, despite wanting to avoid
getting into trouble.

"Are you sure we're doing the right thing here?" Blake asked
Mason, as they made their way through the long corridor
towards Alpha Section.

"If we know him, we can hardly just leave him here, can we?" Mason replied, keeping his eyes on the corridor and the turning up ahead.

"*If* we know him…" Blake said, allowing the sentence to hang in the air.

"I'd hope you wouldn't leave *me* here," Mason said, a little defensively.

"Of course not, but we know that we know you!"

They arrived at Alpha Section and began down the corridor, stopping at the first door on their left.

Upon seeing them, Ven hurried over to the door.

"I never doubted you for a second, Mason!" he lied, clearly filled with joy at seeing them all.

Both Blake and Olivia looked at the face on the other side of the door, trying hard to recognise it, but without success.

Mason attached the device to the door and pressed a button. The gauge on the device registered a certain polarity or strength or whatever it was that Wink had said it would register.

"Is that it?" Blake asked.

Mason pressed another button and stood back, waiting for something to happen, though he wasn't sure quite what to expect.

"Has it worked?" Olivia asked.

"Maybe it takes a moment?"

"Maybe it's broke." Blake guessed.

"If it's a relay device, it will take around three minutes," said Ven, from the other side of the door.

"Seriously?" said Blake. "We just stand here waiting to get caught for three minutes?"

"You'll be fine," said Ven, trying his best to reassure them all. "This corridor sees very slow footfall."

"Oh, well, that's fine then," said Blake, clearly not assured at all.

"How do we know you?" Olivia asked.

"It's a long story," Ven replied.

"Looks like we've got three minutes spare," she said.

Ven took a moment to gather his thoughts. "Right, well, I worked for Zenith, which is this place and then I decided not to work for them, but they didn't like that very much and so I went on the run... but obviously they caught me."

"And that involves us how?"

"We met a few days ago by the river. You took a chip out of my arse and gave me some clothes. Then you took me to stay at Mason's barn so that I could keep out of the way whilst the Bleachers were looking for me. Unfortunately they found me and brought me back here. I scribbled a map, back at the barn, before the Bleachers came back, so that you might find me, if the worst came to the worst, which it did. It was a long shot, banking on the Bleachers leaving the portal open, but they do that quite often, so it was worth a punt, and I'll be honest, I really didn't expect to see you again, but I can't tell you how happy I am that you're here."

"We took a chip out of your arse?" said Olivia.

"Why did you have a chip up your arse?" asked Blake.

"Trust me, we've already done this conversation," Ven replied. "And to be clear, it was in my arse cheek, not actually 'up' my arse."

"Look, I don't want to throw any doubt on all of this," said Olivia, "but we don't remember any of what you just said and so, whilst Mason feels that it's a good idea to set you free, I'm still on the fence."

"I'm also a little bit unsure about this," agreed Blake.

145

"I understand that and I appreciate you all taking a leap of faith," Ven thanked them. "I will help you all get home, I promise."

Part of her wanted to tell him that she didn't think she actually needed his help, but she chose to be cautious and keep the card a secret until she could be sure of his intentions.

There was a loud click from somewhere within the door and the bolt opened. Ven sighed with relief and stepped out of the room and into the hallway.

"You know a quick way out of here?" asked Blake.

"Follow me," said Ven, walking back up the corridor they had just come down.

Before any of them could manage a full stride, they noticed the guards waiting for them.

THIRTY ONE

They hadn't been able to get much out of Irene. They couldn't even be sure that what they had got out of her was real or worth getting at all.

They had asked her if the man from the bin was perhaps just the man that emptied her bins, but she had seemed insistent that he had actually been in her bin and that Blake and Olivia had spoken to the man at some length over coffees.

A homeless person perhaps, although she had said he was dressed fairly smartly, in a shirt and trousers.

They had checked the bin, searched it for clues, but come up empty-handed.

"It's quite likely that they were just helping a homeless guy, buying him a coffee," said Marv, as they wandered up to the allotments at the side of the small park.

"It could also be connected," replied Connor. "A small place like this wouldn't attract many homeless people."

"It's a shame there's no CCTV anywhere around here," Marv said, his eyes skirting his surroundings. "Of course, there's really nothing worth recording and so it would be a complete waste of money."

"It has to be connected," said Connor.

"Does it?"

"Listen. You thought you saw some lights… we go to check them out… we wake up with the mother of all hangovers, with memory problems, in a barn with people we don't know and then those very same people go missing. I would argue that anything remotely strange happening, leading up to those events, has a strong likelihood of being connected."

"You might be right," he agreed, scanning the allotments. "Let's ask this fella if he's seen anything."

They opened the wooden gate and strolled up the narrow path through the gardens to the old man sitting on his deck chair.

"You alright?" he asked.

"I'm Detective Weaving and this is Detective Raines," said Marv, flashing his identification. "I was just wondering if you've seen or heard from either of these two people?"

He handed the photo prints over and Arthur scanned them.

"Are they in trouble?" he asked.

"We're not sure, but they're missing and anything, no matter how insignificant might be helpful in finding them."

"Well, that's Blake and that's Liv," he replied, sensing that these were real investigators, here to help. "I've known them since they were kids."

"When was the last time you saw them?" Marv asked, alert to the lead and finally hopeful of some answers.

"Just the other day. Liv borrowed a metal detector to find a chip in a man's arse."

The detectives were both silent, unsure if they had heard the man correctly.

"A chip?"

"Yeah, they brought him here so I could take it out for him."

"Did you know the man?" Connor asked.

"No, he wasn't from round here. Think they were just helping him out."

"And he had a chip?"

"Yeah, in his arse cheek. I cut it out for him. It seemed odd but the man appeared to be a genuine sort."

"Can you describe the man?" Marv asked.

"Medium height, quite smartly dressed, perhaps mid-forties, cropped hair."

"And did they leave together?" asked Connor, scribbling down notes on to a pad.

"No, he left before them. Thanked us for the help and left. I couldn't tell you where he went."

"And Blake and Olivia?"

"They stayed for another five minutes or so. I assume they were either going home or sometimes they like to pop in to Irene's for a coffee."

"Thanks for your help," said Marv.

"I did see something else too, the other day," Arthur added.

"Okay."

"There was a tall man turned up, asking about the other man. He seemed a bit off to me. Bald head, face like a volleyed cabbage, dressed mostly in black…"

"Smiled a lot?" Marv interrupted, a memory of his own resurfacing.

"Now that you mention it, yeah."

149

"I've seen him," said Marv. "He was asking about a missing friend."

"Thanks for your help," said Connor, as they both started to make their way out of the allotments.

"No problem. Listen, they're good kids. Anything else I can help with, just let me know."

"It's starting to fall into place now," said Marv. "The bald guy is after the other guy, these kids help the other guy and now all three of them are in trouble with the big, bald guy."

"Okay, so we've potentially got a 'why', now we just need a 'where'!"

"Aside from the park, I'm not sure where else to look. We've checked the woods by the barn, there's nothing there - no sign of anything untoward going on…"

"We didn't check the barn itself," said Connor, his eyes lighting up at the prospect.

"We don't really have the authority to check the barn," replied Marv. "Although, we could just ask the mum."

Connor nodded his agreement.

"Let's ask the mum."

THIRTY TWO

They had all been marched away in silence and placed in individual rooms. It was an old tactic that Ven was familiar with, designed to keep people from talking to one another and corroborating each other's stories. He wasn't sure that the others would know that though.

"So, soldiers of your cause have come to your rescue?" said the Bleacher, smiling the same forced smile that they always did.

"What cause?" asked Ven, shaking his head. "There is no cause! I simply decided not to work for the company anymore. People have the right to change their mind!"

The Bleacher laughed. "I think we both know that's not true."

"And that's exactly why I don't want to work here anymore. I used to think we were making righteous decisions and implementing change for the better… for the greater good, but we're not. We seem to be doing the exact opposite in a lot of cases and it's not right."

"Who are you to say what's right and what isn't?" asked the Bleacher.

"Exactly. Who are any of us to say what's right? What was wrong with leaving everything up to Fate?"

"Because Fate is a bitch," spat the Bleacher, angry eyes resting above the forced smile now.

"Is she? Why, because Vitmyre says so? Maybe she's actually kind and approachable and pleasant."

"No, she's a bitch."

"Really?"

"Vitmyre knows."

"Are you sure about that?" Ven asked. "We only have his word that he ever even met Fate, and even if he did, we only have his side of the story. For all we know, maybe he was the arsehole. Have you never questioned the company line?"

"It isn't our place to question…"

"It's everybody's place to question, or else you're just a grey, generic vessel filled with other people's lies and opinions. Is that what you want to be?"

The Bleacher refused to be drawn on the subject and so continued with his own questions.

"What do the others know?"

"Nothing," he replied. He hoped that was the line they were all sticking to.

*

152

Blake was a little unnerved by the tall, smiling, bald man staring back at him from the other side of the room. He supposed this was 'a Bleacher' and he supposed this was an interrogation, possibly like the ones he had seen on the SAS programme on the TV. Those were fairly brutal and involved shouting, stress positions and intimidation, but so far the man had just remained still for a minute and smiled. Still, early days.

"Your name?" asked the Bleacher.

"Blake," he replied. "I'm not sure I'm supposed to be here."

"Oh, that much is certain," the man replied. "Do you know where here is?"

Blake thought for a moment. Best not to give anything away.

"I'm assuming from the yellow sky, it's maybe an aurora? I don't know. Norway? It's not cold enough to be the North Pole."

"I think, perhaps you know it isn't Norway," said the bald man, the smile ever-present on his big face.

"Well, you don't have an accent, so maybe not. I was just guessing really."

"Do you know what this building is?"

"No. I mean, it looks like a factory; a dark, oppressive, windowless factory… Apple?"

"For someone who claims to not know much, you certainly seem to know the man you were trying to break out of the cell."

"Not at all," said Blake, shaking his head. "*He* seemed to know *us* and he seemed quite genuine… very trustworthy face. It felt wrong to just leave him there…"

"Even though the man was clearly locked away for something, you felt it wise to just let him out?"

"I did say *'very'* trustworthy face."

153

"And the device you used to unlock the door?" the Bleacher interrupted.

"If I remember rightly, we found it on the floor."

"I think we both know that's not true."

"I'm just telling you how it happened," Blake protested, hands up in front of him. "The device was on the floor and we wondered what would happen if we attached it to the door. It looked like it might have fallen off at some point. I apologise for trying to fix the place up. You know, your corridors could actually do with a lick of paint here and there too."

*

The Bleacher stared at Mason from across the table, scrutinising the scruffy looking young man from behind the smile.

"Name?"

"Mason Fogg," he replied.

"Why are you here, Mason?"

"I was hoping you could tell me. I don't even know where here is!"

"I'm afraid, I don't believe you," the Bleacher said, softly.

"I can't really be held responsible for your trust issues, man. At some point you're going to have to learn to trust to move forward in life and grow as an individual. You mind if I smoke?"

Mason didn't wait for a reply, but pulled the crooked half-spliff from his pocket and fired it up. It seemed like as good a

154

time as any, and he would hate to be shackled in a dungeon or killed having not smoked it. That would just be wasteful.

"Why are you wearing company uniform?" the Bleacher asked, ignoring the plumes of sweet smoke now forming between them.

"It's kind of embarrassing. I was so scared when we got here that I had an accident in my own clothes and so I had a nose around and found these. I'm sorry, man. I was going to return them. I'm no thief…"

"And yet you also stole a device to free the prisoner?"

"Man, I didn't steal any device. And I merely 'borrowed' the clothes. I'm not sure you're paying attention to my answers; maybe you should write them down."

The smile was beginning to fade from the bald man's face.

"Listen, you can have the clothes back… you might want to wait until I've washed them though."

Mason offered the joint to the Bleacher, who declined.

"I won't tell."

"When did the prisoner recruit you?" the Bleacher asked, ignoring the stoner's attempts at deflection.

"Nobody recruited me. I'm here by mistake. Incidentally, I don't know where here is, but if I'm not home soon, my mum's going to be worried. Last time I went missing for a few days she put posters up everywhere, and I do mean everywhere, so there will be a lot of people out looking for me."

"I'm quite sure they won't find you here. This place isn't exactly easy to find," the Bleacher said, smugness nestling in the smile.

"You say that, but *we're* here," Mason replied, immediately slapping the smugness away, "and we weren't even looking for it."

"So you say."

"It's the truth."

"What has the prisoner told you about his cause?"

Mason scratched at his untidy beard, removing day-old crumbs in the process. Ven's only cause, that he knew of, was to leave a crap job, but it he didn't imagine the man opposite would believe it.

"He never mentioned a cause. Just seemed like he wanted to leave your shitty company. Have you thought about just letting him leave?"

"I would be more worried about your own predicament. You're going to be here a long time, if we don't start getting answers." The Bleacher stared hard at him, as he took the last drag on his smoke.

*

Olivia looked the man up and down, disapprovingly and though the Bleacher seemed unperturbed, he did feel a little smaller under her gaze.

"Let's start with your name," said the bald man.

"Let's start with my phone call," said Olivia.

"Excuse me?"

"I'm entitled to a phone call. And while we're at it, if you're arresting me, you have to tell me what you're arresting me for."

"I don't know what you think this is," the Bleacher started, "but I can assure you, we are not the police and we don't have to give you a phone call. You have no rights here and no entitlements."

"What sort of place is this?" she asked, disgusted at how the man was speaking to her, though in truth, she was expecting things to get much worse.

"There are only two reasons why you are here... either by design or by mistake."

"Well, I can assure you it is by mistake!" Olivia exclaimed.

"Mistakes are erased," came the rather blunt reply.

"Oh. And if it were by design?" she fished.

"Then there would be many questions to answer."

That sounded marginally better than being erased. Perhaps if she knew something, she would be useful. Knowledge was power, so the saying went. That being said, she didn't really know anything, but they didn't know that. On the contrary, they actually believed that she did know something and so all she really had to do was play to that.

"Let's say maybe I do know a few things. I want some assurances before I tell you anything," she said, playing her bluff.

"You're not exactly in a position to demand anything," replied the Bleacher.

"I'm entirely in a position to demand things. I know things, important things that you want to know, but my friends and I want to go home, so you make that happen and maybe I spill the beans."

"Or maybe we torture you until you tell us anyway?"

"I'm likely to just tell you any old rubbish if you do that!" she said, stifling a panicked laugh. "Haven't you heard how unreliable information gained by torture actually is? It's common knowledge. I'm likely to tell you that Santa Claus exists if I'm being tortured, whereas, the civil way..."

157

A guard knocked on the door and entered, giving Olivia a contemptuous look before locking on to the Bleacher.

"They are to be readied for trial."

The Bleacher looked a little surprised. "But we have barely begun…"

"The big man wants it done. He's overseeing the proceedings himself."

Olivia tried to gauge the strained expression on the bald man's face. Difficult as it was to draw a comprehensive conclusion, she decided to assume it wasn't good news.

THIRTY THREE

The Bleachers had left the rooms, leaving the guards to take the prisoners to the court room. It looked every bit like a court they had seen on television; dark wood panelling, pews on either side of the aisle, presumably one side for the defence and the other for the prosecution and the judge's bench at the front.

The guards ushered them all into a pew to the right of the aisle, Mason and then Olivia, Blake and Ven. He told them to sit and wait.

Blake stared at the guards facing them, stood either side of the judge's bench, stoic and angry looking. Maybe they were bred that way, genetically pissed off and fed to a point where they were two sizes too big for their uniform.

He turned to Olivia, next to him.

"It's just us," he said.

"Who else are you expecting?" she whispered her reply.

"A lawyer?" he shrugged. "Maybe a prosecution team, a jury…"

"It doesn't work like that here," said Ven, overhearing their conversation. "It's just one judge, usually one of the bigwigs."

He was shocked then to see the old man himself, Vitmyre stroll into the room and step up behind the bench.

"Holy shit, that's Vitmyre," he said, under his breath.

A relatively slight man, his white hair and beard and the lines on his face hinted at his grand old age, though he was walking unaided and at a relatively quick pace. He was wearing yellow pyjamas with small, brown teddy bears printed on them and smoking a pipe as he took his seat at the head of the courtroom. An advisor stood close behind him.

He looked down at the prisoners and eyed them one by one, squinting until he reached Ven.

"It is late and I haven't had my bath," he paused and looked over his shoulder to his advisor. "Have I?" he asked.

"You did have that one earlier," he replied gently, almost apologetically, not wanting to disagree with the boss. "But, you certainly haven't had 'second bath time' and it's not particularly early," he crawled.

Vitmyre returned his attention to the prisoners.

"So, you're the trespassers. I thought you'd all be taller," he remarked, his gravelled tones those of a man who had smoked a pipe for many a year.

"They're sat down, sir," said the advisor, leaning in, tentatively.

"Makes sense. It's a long way to get here. I couldn't walk it, not in these boots. I'm not even sure they're mine. Are these my boots?" he asked the advisor.

160

"Yes," he nodded. "Certainly since you took them from that boy."

Blake and Olivia shared a glance. It relayed much in the way of confusion.

"Well, let's get on with it, shall we?" he said, coughing to clear his throat. "I'm a little disappointed, Ven."

"I'm sure you are, sir," he replied. "Truth is, so am I."

"How so?"

"I've been spun a lie, about this place, about what we do here. I was led to believe we were doing some good, steering the course of nations, affecting real change…"

"And you don't think we've done that?" Vitmyre asked.

"No. A month ago you had me make a course correction that resulted in an entire village being crushed by stampeding wildebeest. How is that possibly a good thing?"

"Well now, everything is good from at least one point of view. Imagine how wonderful that must have felt for the wildebeest. Didn't we keep a few of them as a reminder?" he asked the advisor.

"Just a couple of hooves, as I recall."

"Oh. Well, I do vaguely remember that particular course correction and as I recall, the government of that country needed that land for its oil reserves. Laws prohibited them from digging for oil with a human populous there and they couldn't just take the land…"

Ven sat, stunned at the explanation. "That's exactly what I'm talking about. That's horrible."

"I agree, it was a little messy, but you have to think about the bigger picture."

"That being?"

"We did that little favour for that country and we gained vital supplies in return. Water, gold… I don't know if you've seen it

161

outside, but we're not exactly rich in resources here. Our particular universal pocket seems to be sorely lacking in water and we can't just let people die of thirst, can we? And the factory needs gold to produce the portals. If we can't keep producing new portals, how can we stay in the game?"

"But it's not a game, this is people's lives!"

"Come now, let's not be naïve. For some to gain, some have to lose. It's a matter of balance."

"It seems like a remarkably skewed balance."

"Certainly," Vitmyre agreed. "In our favour. There's nothing wrong with that."

"Even if it's at the expense of innocent lives?"

"Listen" the old man began, "I once had a boat... had a monkey in it and everything and then one day I couldn't find the boat. I looked everywhere for it and then..." he took a puff on his pipe, "the monkey told me he had swapped it for a flute and a bag of daisies."

The advisor leaned in. "I think that may have been a dream, sir," he whispered.

"So, I don't have a flute?" Vitmyre asked.

"Not that I know of, sir."

"Do I still have a boat?"

"I don't think so."

"What about the monkey?"

"I'll have someone look into it, sir."

"Good. Don't want that sneaky son of a bitch stealing all of my things. Better put a guard on my boat too, just in case."

Ven looked on, as did Blake, Olivia and Mason, astounded that the man in front of them was running things. He clearly had just a handful of marbles left and they were quickly running out.

"I've got a question," Olivia announced. "What is going on here?"

"It looks like we're in court," said Vitmyre. "I'm assuming you've done something wrong."

"I mean with this place. What is it, what is Zenith?"

This seemed to bring back memories for the old man and his eyes once again sparkled with purpose.

"Zenith is a new tomorrow," he said with vigour, impassioned with renewed belief.

"Could you elaborate on that?" she asked.

"I was young once, just like you, full of ideas and energy, bound to a job that I loved, but with great new ideas about how to innovate and modernise the industry…"

"What industry?" she asked.

"Destiny. The art of governing worlds, of writing the stories and steering the course of history." He paused for a moment, puffing on the pipe and searching his memories.

"Pretty big stuff, man," said Mason, under his breath.

"Generally speaking, Fate governs your neck of the woods," the old man said, looking at Olivia, Blake and Mason in turn. "She has quite the monopoly, you might say, but then there are only a handful of beings capable of dealing with that amount of knowledge. I mean, imagine knowing all of the possible outcomes for everyone and everything and keeping all of those plates spinning in the right direction. Not an easy job, right?"

Mason nodded, heavily engrossed in the story and still a little stoned.

"But why do we need anyone steering our destinies at all?" Blake asked.

"Well, that's an easy one," scoffed the advisor. "The universe, left to its own devices, would see everything crumble, decay and dissipate into nothing. The human race would have

163

destroyed itself on a number of occasions by now, if it hadn't been for the likes of us, because just as the universe seems determined to eat itself to death, so too are humans drawn to a similar path."

"So, you actually worked for Fate?" Ven asked the old man.

"I did. And I could have helped her too. Always one to push the boundaries, I created a bio-algorithm that would allow others to shoulder some of the burden, to lighten her workload."

"Others?" Ven asked.

"Well, me," Vitmyre replied. "A non-God."

"I'm guessing she didn't like the idea?"

"No. I had to steal some of her essence in order for the algorithm to really kick into gear and let's just say she wasn't overly pleased about that. I escaped from the realm and I've been here ever since, apart from that short trip to the beach to look for giant smoking crabs."

"Also a dream, sir," the advisor mumbled close to his ear.

"And so you set up Zenith?" asked Blake.

"I did. A small outfit to begin with, but it has gotten progressively bigger over time. Big enough now so that she finally takes us seriously!" he stood, defiantly.

"So, this is all just to get back at the boss lady for rejecting your idea?" Olivia said, stunned at the realisation.

"My idea works!" the old man exclaimed. "She said it couldn't be done, that a non-God couldn't possibly cope with the weight of knowledge needed for the task. I've proven otherwise."

"At what cost?" asked Ven.

"People die," said Vitmyre. "It is inevitable. But why should only Gods be allowed to write those ends?"

"Maybe that's just the natural order of things," said Olivia.

164

"To Hell with the natural order!" he banged his fist on the bench. "And to Hell with anybody who can't see beyond it! The natural order would have it all end in nothingness and we can't have that."

The advisor clapped. "Quite right, sir."

"So, now what?" the old man asked, looking lost again.

"Now we need to sentence the trespassers."

"Hang on!" Olivia called out. "We haven't even presented the defence yet."

"That's not really how this works," said the advisor.

The old man stood and brought his pipe down on the bench a few times, demanding quiet in the room.

"I hereby find the four of you guilty," he eventually said.

"Of what?" said Olivia, disgusted at the lack of justice.

"Release the sharks!" called Vitmyre, his voice thunderous, the delivery bordering on theatrical.

"Erm, we don't have any sharks, sir," said the advisor.

"Oh. What do we have?"

"We normally send people to the erasing cages."

"Fine," the old man shook his head and started to walk off. "Do that then. Now, about my boat…"

He trailed off as he left the room, the advisor shuffling after him, leaving the four of them stunned, Ven perhaps less so than the others.

"What just happened?" asked Mason.

"I'm not sure exactly," replied Blake, "but it wasn't good."

"What are erasing cages?" Olivia asked.

"You're hung in cages over a 'wasting void', where you're basically erased from existence over the course of a week," said Ven, as the guards ordered them all to rise and fall into line in the aisle.

"Well, that's lovely."

165

THIRTY FOUR

The erasing cages were ancient-looking, wrought-iron, barred boxes, suspended from a reinforced concrete ceiling, twenty feet high above a huge, seemingly bottomless chasm in the ground, some twenty feet across.

They had been marched up a concrete staircase, which clung to the walls, to a platform and made to wait, as a guard reeled in the cages, one by one, attached as they were by great clunking chains to the mechanisms. Once in the individual cages, they were reeled out again and left swaying over the dark void, the creaking of the metal an eerie echo to their desperate fate.

"Well, isn't this nice?" said Olivia, as the last guard left the huge room, slamming the iron door shut behind them.

"I'm not a fan, if I'm honest," said Mason, from his own cage, swinging gently in the dark.

"I was being sarcastic," she said, feeling as if she was about to break down in tears. "I can't believe it ends like this."

"It won't end like this," Blake tried to comfort her.

"Really? Have you got a plan?"

He hadn't and so kept quiet. He glanced over at Ven's cage, though it was difficult to see beyond the bars of his own, such was the level of darkness in the chamber.

"What's down there anyway?" he eventually called over to Ven.

"A yellow hole, or so I'm led to believe," he replied.

"A yellow hole?" Blake asked. "It doesn't look very yellow."

"Well, it looks black to us, but the true colour is yellow, according to the experts."

"Is it like a black hole?" asked Mason.

"Much smaller, much yellower and I think it works in a slightly different way, but essentially it isn't that far off. Third cousin, twice removed sort of thing. That's what will be vacuuming us out of existence over the next week or so."

"How did they get a black hole inside a building?" Blake asked, struggling to comprehend the science.

"It's a yellow hole; they're not that rare and they're relatively easy to catch... apparently."

"I can't believe this is happening," Olivia said, quietly, almost to herself, although the others heard her.

"This is all my fault," said Ven.

"I agree," she said quickly. "If we hadn't stopped to get you out, we could have been away."

"It's my fault for getting you involved in the first place. I should never have drawn the map. Once the Bleachers had been to the barn, I just drew it as a back-up..." he trailed off,

167

letting the words fall to the darkness, wishing that the memory wipe injection had worked on him. He had been exposed to it several times over the years and any effects had only ever been short-lived, even in those early days. He supposed he would forget everything soon enough anyway, once the erasing really took hold.

They sat in silence for a while; each of them lost to their memories of family, friends, even the more regular and mundane aspects of their lives.

Blake couldn't help but think about some of the things he hadn't done yet, which was almost everything. Aside from Call Of Duty and a few other games, he hadn't really done much at all. He hadn't even managed to see Jim's new band play at The Griffin yet.

Olivia was lost in a sea of faces that she would no longer get to see, her parents, her younger sister, The Onion Sage and even Irene. And then she began to regret any time she had wasted; learning French when she had no intention of ever going there, those countless hours slaving over the cheese assignments, even the hour watching Jim's new band at The Griffin. *Especially* the hour watching Jim's new band.

Mason was no longer stoned. Impending death had seen to that. He couldn't make his mind up whether he was more annoyed at the lack of aliens or at the fact that he was going to die. He settled on being angry at dying without having seen any aliens.

Ven had never been the type to wallow in self-pity. Things went wrong all the time, such was life. It was about how you dealt with things going wrong that counted; how you dusted yourself off and ploughed on regardless. Usually. Even he had to admit to himself that this time seemed a little different, a little more final.

168

"Any chance you think Fate might give us a hand out of this one?" Blake asked Ven.

"She doesn't have any jurisdiction here," Ven replied.

"I thought that might be a lot to ask for," he sighed.

"I don't suppose there's an appeals process?" Olivia asked.

Ven shook his head and although she couldn't make him out in the dark, she didn't need to. She had already known the answer before the words had left her mouth.

"Man, your boss is a complete shit," said Mason, thinking about the old man and the 'trial'.

"Yeah, I think you were right to try and get out," agreed Blake.

"Didn't work out very well though, did it?" said Ven, shaking his head.

They heard the latch on the metal door twenty feet or so beneath them.

"I hope this is some food, I'm starving," said Mason.

It was only one set of feet coming up the concrete stairs and as the group looked over towards the platform, they were surprised to see Wink looking back at them.

"Wink!" said Blake, hopeful for a moment.

"Wink?" said Ven. "What are you doing here?"

"It's not right, what they've done," he replied. "Me and you go way back. You've always been good with me, helped me out when those supplies went missing, and when that pump exploded... thought I was for the can then."

He looked around at the other cages, big eyes staring back.

"And these guys... they could have gone. They'd forgotten who you were and they had an out, but they didn't take it. They did the right thing and now I need to do the right thing too."

He pulled a lever on the wall and the huge chain started to pull Ven's cage towards the platform.

169

"Thank you so much," Ven said, the cage swaying and squeaking with the momentum.

"We need to hurry," Wink urged. "I told the guards I had to change a couple of bolts on the mechanisms. That will only buy us about ten minutes."

One by one, Wink pulled in the cages and each of the group made their way down the steps and waited at the bottom, just feet away from the enormous hole in the ground, nervous of its silent power.

Wink joined them at the bottom of the stairs.

"Is everyone alright?" he asked.

"I think so," said Mason. Everybody else nodded, eager to hear the next plan of action.

"You hide behind the wall in the corner. I'll call the guards in… tell them the cages are empty and that the yellow hole must be growing bigger to have erased you in such a short space of time. That will cause a panic. You should be able to sneak out in the confusion."

"Thank you, Wink," said Ven.

"Have you still got the card?" he asked Olivia.

"Yeah, it's in my sock."

"Come with us," said Ven.

"I'm not sure it would be my cup of tea over there," Wink smiled. "Besides, I'm going to try and force a few changes around here."

"Really?" asked Ven. "How are you going to do that?"

"In about an hour, I'm going to attach a pop flare inside the power generator and trip the whole network; cause a black out. That should upset the flow of things for a day or two."

"Okay," said Ven, smiling inwardly at the thought of Vitmyre and his cronies losing their shit. "And then?"

170

"Well, that's as far as I've got." He smiled. "You need to be out of here before I do that. It'll stop the portals from working."

Mason scratched at his unkempt beard. "Why don't you make that plan a bit more permanent?" he asked.

"How do you mean?" Wink seemed confused.

"Take out the portals for good," Mason elaborated.

"There's not a lot of resources over here. Truth is, we rely on the portals, wouldn't have much without them. They're not the problem."

"Vitmyre's the problem," said Ven.

"He's old, losing his marbles…" said Wink. "Besides, we're not the only ones who are unhappy with the way things are run around here. It won't be long before somebody else takes the reins. Now, let's get you out of here."

"Thanks again," said Ven.

"You're a good man," said Olivia.

"Good enough," he smiled back. "Everyone hide. Let's do this."

THIRTY FIVE

Marv tried the door to the barn and it opened with ease. He peered in, glancing first at the kitchen to the right and then through to the main room, via the small corridor.

"I'm surprised it isn't locked," replied Mason's mum, who had accompanied the detectives, armed with a spare key to let them in.

Connor followed them both in. There was no sign of a struggle, the detectives noted, nothing that immediately raised the alarm.

"Does this seem usual, Mrs Fogg?" Connor asked, gesturing to the living area in general.

"I think so. I don't really pay much attention to it, if I'm honest. I do his washing, but I draw the line at being his maid. There is normally a general untidiness to the place, so this seems fairly typical."

Marv looked over to the muddle of computer towers, screens and wires in the corner of the room. It looked like a fairly scattershot set-up, but he was hardly the expert when it came to technology. He was usually a good decade or so behind the curve; still collecting CDs when others were streaming music, still using an actual camera when others were using their phones. Technology simply moved too quickly for him.

"Does this seem usual?" Marv asked the lady.

"I've no idea," she shrugged. "I haven't got a clue with all that sort of thing."

"That makes two of us," Marv said. "I wouldn't know a megabyte from a… well…" He didn't feel it necessary to finish the sentence, safe in the knowledge that she had understood the point he had been trying to make.

It took only another two minutes to go through the place, Mrs Fogg assuring them at every stage that it all seemed 'usual' or at the very least, usual for Mason.

They stepped back outside and stared at the remnants of vomit still decorating the ground.

"That's not usual," she said, locking the door behind them.

"Those blue lights you saw," Marv said, quickly changing the subject. "Do you know in which part of the woods they would have been?"

She considered it for a moment. "Fairly central. Have you had a wander through?"

"Just a quick one, earlier" Connor replied.

"Maybe somewhere around the clearing with the tyre swing. Did you see that?"

"We did."

"I'd come with you, but I've got a cake in the oven," she explained, somewhat sheepishly. "I'll go and see to it and just let me know when you're done."

173

Marv thanked her for her help and assured her that they would be fine going in alone, although he didn't like the look of the darkening clouds, threatening rain and the lack of sleep wasn't exactly helping his mood either.

THIRTY SIX

It had gone according to plan.

Wink had called the two guards into the chamber and explained how it simply shouldn't have been possible for the prisoners to have been erased in such a short space of time and that the only explanation was that the yellow hole must have grown exponentially over the last few hours and that in itself was extremely dangerous and posed a significant threat to the whole facility.

The group had very carefully crept out through the door, as Wink had shown the guards up the stairs to witness the empty cages.

They had hurried through the dull corridors, pausing to peek around every corner before continuing, hearts beating faster as they went.

They heard a group of guards running a little further down one of the corridors and so squeezed into a tight concrete stairwell, just off a corridor, waiting for any danger to pass.

"Wait a minute," said Blake. "The lie that Wink used about the yellow hole… well, Vitmyre will know that isn't the truth, won't he?"

"Not for a good while," said Ven. "His 'special knowledge' is pretty much confined to 'your side', the same as it is for Fate. After all, what knowledge he has was stolen from her in the first place."

"He might guess though," said Olivia.

"He might," Ven agreed, "though his brain seems a little preoccupied with boats and monkeys at the minute. In any case, we need to hurry up and get out of here."

They listened out for the guards passing in the corridor.

"If his knowledge is focused on 'our side', won't he know exactly where we are when we get there?" asked Mason.

There was silence then, apart from the noise of the guards in the corridor beyond, as they all thought on what Mason had said.

"Wait. You're right," said Olivia.

"Am I?" Mason seemed stunned that his musing had foundation.

"He uses trackers on employees, it's just quicker, but you're right, he has an in-depth knowledge of everyone on your side," Ven grudgingly agreed. "I have a place to go to though. It's impossible for him to reach."

"Really?" asked Olivia. "If you can get there, why couldn't he?"

"He doesn't know that it exists."

"Where is it?" she asked.

176

"It's another pocket," Ven revealed. "Aside from the business of destiny, Vitmyre had some of us searching for evidence of other pocket universes. He's not exactly smitten with this place... there's hardly any water, no gold to power the portals, it's tiny as far universes go; even the views are shit."

"When were you planning on telling us all this?" Olivia asked.

"I'd hoped it wouldn't be necessary for you to know about it, thought I would be on my way by now and not need to bother anyone and then... well, once we got caught it just seemed irrelevant. We were going to die!" he added, defensively.

"So either we come with you to a new pocket universe or Vitmyre will find us?" said Blake.

"You'd be safe there," Ven replied, keen to highlight the positives.

"What about our families?"

"They could come too."

"Believe it or not, they might not want to just uproot their lives, at the drop of a hat to live in another universe, Ven," Olivia said, her voice filled with irritation. "They have jobs, friends..."

"I'm sorry. I had no way of knowing it would come to this, I just wanted you to get a chip out of my arse. I shouldn't have accepted your help, shouldn't have drawn the map, but there were signs..."

"Signs?" Blake asked.

"Signs that Fate was intervening... a white carrier bag at the allotment, a white dove on the roof of the barn. She was pointing the way."

"How do you know it wasn't just a regular carrier bag?" asked Mason.

177

"I just know. It's how she communicates with me. Sometimes it's a white cat, other times... well, it can be anything, but it's always white and it always catches my eye."

"That's lovely and everything," Olivia interrupted, "but maybe we should decide what we are doing and get out of the stairwell, before we get caught again."

"Maybe we should see if Wink needs some help?" Blake suggested.

They all looked at him.

"You want to stay?" asked Ven.

"Not really, but if our other options are going home only to be tracked down again or moving to another universe, then I'm willing to consider other suggestions. I'm quite partial to the universe I grew up in, despite not really paying much attention to it."

"We only have a short amount of time to get out of here," said Ven. "Once Wink sets off that flare, the portals will be out of action."

Olivia sighed. "Blake's right. Listen, I'm completely up for getting out of here and going home, but if they are just going to catch us again, what's the point? And I'm sorry, Ven, moving to another universe isn't really going to work for me."

They all looked at Mason.

"I'm actually quite keen on checking out another universe," he said, defensively. "But I'm also always up for bringing down the establishment," he added. "Especially when the establishment is being run by a corrupt dinosaur who is all of the rides short of a theme park."

"Right," Ven said, searching his soul for the correct course.

Initially, his plan had been to just leave the company. He had known that it would be difficult, but having found the 'other place', had assured himself that he would be beyond the company's reach. But the signs had led him this far. Fate had wanted him to meet Blake and Olivia and Mason, of that much he was certain and if they wanted to bring down the company, then maybe that was what Fate wanted too.

"Ven?" Blake prompted.

"Okay," he said. "What's your plan?"

Blake looked on, still for a moment as the realisation kicked in. "I don't have one," he finally replied. "I was rather hoping you might."

"My plan was to get out of here," he said.

"Okay, well, I suppose if Vitmyre is the problem, we need to get rid of Vitmyre."

"And by 'get rid of' you mean...?"

Blake wasn't sure what he meant, hadn't thought anything through at all.

"I mean, make not there anymore."

"Kill him?" asked Ven.

"I'm not sure about that..." Blake protested.

"Ask him politely to retire... lock him in a box...?"

"I don't know," Blake eventually conceded. "I've no idea. I'm not the secret agent here. I suppose I thought you might have a few ideas up your sleeve after years of covert operations."

"I do know he's up on the fifth floor, has a huge suite up there," Ven began, "but there are guards outside. We'd need a distraction."

Mason grinned.

179

THIRTY SEVEN

They took the stairwell to the fifth floor. It seemed to get darker the higher they went, though that might have been their own minds playing tricks on them.

"Okay, so your idea is…" said Olivia, trying to comprehend the absurdity of it.

"I put ketchup on my face and run at the guards, telling them I've been attacked…"

"Where did you get ketchup from?" asked Blake.

"I always have ketchup," said Mason, as if it were the most normal thing in the world.

"You always have ketchup on you? Why?"

"I take it from cafes and takeaways, mayonnaise too." He unzipped the Waste Department overalls and unbuttoned his shirt pocket underneath, before pulling out a handful of sachets.

"Why do you carry them around with you?" asked Ven.

"I'll be honest, I got these from the takeaway the other week and I haven't washed this shirt since…" he thought for a moment, "well, I'm not sure I've ever washed this shirt."

"Ew," Olivia said, looking at him with disgust.

"It's alright, I put Febreeze on it," he explained.

"That's not what that's for," she said, shaking her head.

"So, you're going to just go up to the guards and what?" asked Blake.

"Tell them we are under attack and erm… maybe they need re-enforcements downstairs?" Mason seemed a little unsure of his own plan, hastily thrown together as it was just a few moments ago.

The looks he got back seemed equally uncertain, but nobody had any better plans.

"It's worth a shot," said Ven, eventually.

"Okay," said Blake. Olivia shrugged her agreement and Mason began to apply the ketchup to his left eyebrow and around the dark hairline by his left ear.

"How does it look?" Mason asked.

"Actually quite convincing," said Olivia, surprised.

"Now, you just need to seem panicked," said Ven. "Lead the guards to the elevator and we'll head straight into the old man's suite."

"I'll tell them I'm too scared to go with them," said Mason, "because of the wound and everything."

"We won't have long before they realise there's no attack, two or three minutes, perhaps," Ven explained. "We'll need to be quick."

They all acknowledged their understanding and Mason opened the door to the fifth floor and left the others waiting in the stairwell.

181

He hurried along the corridor, before turning right and spotting the two guards by the door.

"Oh, thank God," said Mason, in his best 'alarmed' voice. "We're under attack…"

"From what?" asked the female guard.

"Something…" Mason replied. "Something from the yellow hole?" It was more of a question than anything. "They need back-up over in the Erasing chamber!"

"We're not supposed to leave…" she started.

"They need everyone capable down there to help – all hands on deck!"

She didn't look wholly convinced.

"We can't leave the door unguarded," the male guard said.

"Go, I'll keep watch by the door!"

The two guards looked at each other briefly before rushing down the corridor, nudging Mason as they went.

"Use the elevator!" he called after them.

Ven heard them run by the door to the stairwell and on towards the elevator. He waited until he heard the lift doors close before whispering over to Blake and Olivia, as they waited on his word.

"Let's go," he said.

They followed him, darting quickly along the corridor, before turning to see Mason opening the door to the suite. They caught up with him and followed just behind.

The room was as luxurious as you would expect, spacious, mood lighting throughout, high ceilings, plush furniture, grand piano in the corner, small inflatable paddling pool in the centre of the living room.

Vitmyre walked into the room, wearing a string vest and a pair of bright yellow knee-length shorts. Around his waist sat an inflatable ring with the head of a giraffe. He looked a little surprised to see them.

"Can I help you?" he asked, pausing a moment from peeling a banana.

"We need to move you, sir," said Ven.

"But I've not had my paddle yet."

"I'm afraid paddle time has been cancelled, sir. It's quite urgent."

The old man looked at Ven with a flicker of recognition.

"Ven, isn't it?"

"Yes, sir."

"I thought you'd gone to prison or something?"

"I got released," he said. "Good behaviour."

"Good," the old man replied, before continuing to peel the banana. "However, I'm afraid I can't miss paddle time, Ven. I've put my boots on and everything."

"We've found your boat," said Blake, sensing the time slipping away from them.

"Oh, excellent!" the old man enthused. "And the monkey?"

"Not sure about that," Blake replied.

"Ah, he's a crafty old sod, that monkey. Beat me at Poker, you know?" the old man rambled. "At least, I think it was Poker. What's the thing with a shuttle cock?"

"We need to go now if we want to get the boat," Ven urged.

"Very well," Vitmyre ceded, taking a bite of the banana before tossing the rest of it into the paddling pool.

He joined the group as they left the suite and headed for the stairwell.

"Please tell me you know a good way out of here," said Olivia, just behind Ven as they descended the concrete steps.

"I do," Ven replied. "We can get out at the bottom of the

stairwell; opens up into a warehouse and there's a door out of there that leads over to the portals."

They followed Ven, checking the coast was clear from the stairwell before entering the immense warehouse.

There, they headed down one of the aisles, flanked by ten feet high metal shelves, crammed full with boxes and crates.

"I don't think I've ever been in here," said the old man, bewildered by the scale of the place. "What's in all the boxes?"

"Paperwork," said Ven, keeping a beady eye out as he led the pack. "The whole place is just one big account of everything you have ever sanctioned; every course correction in detail, every lead we ever looked into, every portal opened, every explored avenue… essentially, everything you know."

"I know a good deal more than this," he scoffed. "I have to know almost everything there is to know. That's what the job is. Knowing things."

"Did you ever feel like the weight of all that knowledge was just a bit too much?" Ven asked, careful not to insinuate that the old man was clearly losing his grip on reality.

"The first time I drank from the essence…"

"The essence that you took from Fate?" Ven asked.

"Yes. It hit me like a sledgehammer." His eyes widened at the memory of it. "All that knowledge all at once… she had been right. It's not meant for a non-God. I was sick, felt like my head had exploded… all of a sudden I was aware of where everybody was, what they were doing and to a large degree, why they were doing it, but none of them were from our own universe."

"Just from the other side?" said Ven.

"Yes, the non-divine side. The Gods call it the lower plain."

"So you're from a universe of Gods?" asked Mason.

184

"I suppose so," the old man said, still taking in the world of paperwork surrounding him.

"But you're not a God?" asked Blake.

"No, always fancied a go at it though," he smiled now and something of the younger version of him simmered behind his eyes again. "Why should they have all the fun?"

"Why do they even have all this knowledge about our side?" Olivia asked. "What even is a God?"

"That's something I don't know," confessed the old man. "It was just a given that the Gods dealt with the destinies of the 'other' universe. I simply asked the question 'What's so special about Gods?'"

"What is she like, Fate?" asked Ven, pausing for a moment before looking over to the door in the far corner of the warehouse.

"I can barely remember any more," he said, trying desperately for a memory that probably no longer existed. "Anyway, about this boat…"

"We'll get you to it," Ven assured him.

They crossed an open floor to the metal door. Ven paused before opening it up, slowly. He peered out on to the dark ground, quiet under the familiar gritty yellow sky and then on down towards the almost never-ending line of portals, all unique scenes disappearing off into the distance.

"Is the boat outside?" asked Vitmyre.

"It's not far," Ven replied, stepping out on to the gravel.

The others followed, Vitmyre and then Blake, Olivia and Mason.

They snaked their way through a circuit of gravel paths. All of them, apart from Vitmyre, were looking out for Bleachers or guards as they went. It took only a few minutes to reach the tyre swing.

Olivia removed the polarity card from her sock and handed it to Ven, who tapped it on to the tyre. There was a warm hum that followed, as if a machine had booted into life.

"Blake, you go first," said Ven.

He took a deep breath and sat himself down. It wasn't long before the blue orbs claimed him and he was gone.

"Sir, if you don't mind," Ven gestured for the old man to take a seat, which he did so.

"Oh, that tickles…" he said as Ven noticed the three Bleachers making their way over to them.

THIRTY EIGHT

"What's a silent rave?" asked Marv.

"It's like a regular rave, but instead of the music being blared out on speakers, everyone has headphones on," Connor replied.

"And that's real, is it? That's an actual thing?"

"Yeah."

"And you think that's what might have happened here?"

"The mum said she saw lights, but there was no noise," he held up his hands. "It's just a thought."

"It's not a very good thought," said Marv, kicking through the dark grass, shining his pocket torch all around, illuminating the ground in the dying light.

"Well, I'm just struggling to marry up the blue lights with the 'man on the run' theory…"

"And you think a silent rave is the answer?"

They both continued looking around the treeline, occasionally glancing up at the tyre swing and then at each other, with defeated expressions.

"Maybe there is no connection?" posited Connor.

Blue orbs began to emerge from within the tyre swing, floating out into the darkening glade.

"Oh shit," said Marv.

"Oh shit," repeated Connor.

And then Blake was there, rising to a stand and walking away from the tyre. He spotted them, gawping back at him.

"Hey. You're the detectives, right?" he asked, recalling them from earlier.

They could barely scrape together syllables to make a sound, but Marv managed a bewildered 'yeah'.

"Thought so. You are not going to believe the day we've had!"

"Probably not," agreed Marv.

And then the old man was through, birthed from out of the tyre amongst a flurry of blue lights, all string vest, shorts and pale legs.

"Wow. Very fizzy," he smiled, enjoying the sensation. "I'd forgotten what that felt like."

He wandered slowly over to Blake, taking in the surrounding dark woods under the evening sky. Having seen the old man come through, Blake fully realised just how strange it must have looked to the two bewildered detectives, whose bafflement had been momentarily illuminated by the blue lights.

"You're probably wondering what's going on," he said.

"I wouldn't mind an explanation, just when you've got a minute," said Marv.

188

Another bustle of lights lit up the glade and Olivia appeared, panicked, followed almost immediately by Mason.

"We need to get out of here," she said, doing her best to ignore the fizzing sensation washing through her body. "Bleachers will be through any moment!"

"Shit," said Blake.

Ven arrived just seconds later. "Run, quickly!" he shouted.

They all did so, the detectives joining them, with no real understanding as to why they were running, what Bleachers were or what in general was going on, but their brains were going through something of a reboot and they had at least found the missing people. It was better that they kept tabs on them, even if solely from a career point of view.

Blake was leading the way, although Mason had made his way to the side of him and in truth it was Blake who was being led. Mason knew the woods better than anyone and so it seemed sensible to keep an eye on where he was going. Olivia followed Blake, with Ven keeping a few feet behind the old man, so as to keep an eye on him. He wasn't sure why they were running, but was doing well to keep up with those at the front. Marv and Connor brought up the rear and both turned to see another burst of blue lights behind them, through the trees. They didn't allow their eyes to linger on the scene. Perhaps, amongst all of the weirdness and panic, they didn't want to see what they were running from.

It took no longer than two or three minutes to get to the barn and to the detective's car.

"Is this yours?" Blake asked Marv, although he was almost certain it didn't belong to anyone else.

"Yeah."

"We need to get out of here…" he began.

"I doubt we'll fit everyone in," said Marv.

189

Blake had already opened the back door and was busy ushering Olivia and the old man inside.

"Okay," said Marv, realising it was all happening anyway.

"I'll drive," said Connor, opening the driver's door and sitting inside.

After Blake had sat next to the old man, who was in the middle of the back seats, Mason climbed in and sat on Olivia's lap and Ven followed suit on the other side, squashing down on to Blake's lap. Marv jumped in the front passenger seat and the car was reversing away from the barn before he had even closed his door.

Connor struggled to see through the rear windscreen, crammed as the back seat was.

"Jesus, your arse is bony," Olivia said to Mason.

"Sorry, if I could move it, I would."

Marv saw the tall men bounding free of the woods, sinister smiles, dark eyes fixed on the car, on their prey.

"Shit!" he called out and all eyes in the car were looking outwards in alarm.

Connor turned the wheel quickly, reversing out on to the road, before changing gear and slamming his foot on the accelerator. The engine roared its displeasure, never before having been called upon to produce a quick getaway, but the car was up to the task and pulled away from the Bleachers, though they still gave chase, one of them throwing what looked like a stone at the car, but only managing to hit the rear bumper.

They all managed a sigh of relief, but it would take much longer for their heartbeats to slow.

"That was close," said Blake, wiping the worry from his forehead.

"They'll just keep coming," said Ven.

"Who are they?" asked Marv. "What sort of trouble are you in?"

They all looked at each other, none of them wanting the unenviable task of explaining.

"Well, that was fun," said Vitmyre. "Much better than paddling. Now, about my boat…"

THIRTY NINE

They pulled up across from the chapel and Connor turned the engine off, so that they were sat in the dark.

"Okay," said Marv, turning in his chair to face the crowded backseat. "So, you're saying you're from another universe?"

"Yes," said Ven.

"And you write the destinies of mankind?"

"Well, not me personally," said Ven. "This man is the head of the operation," he nodded to Vitmyre, sat next to him.

"He's your boss?"

"Was. I recently retired."

"I know I just saw you all come through a magic tyre swing, but this is still pretty difficult to swallow."

"Detective, I wonder if you've seen my boat?" said the old man.

"You've lost a boat?" asked Connor.

"A monkey stole it."

"I'm not sure Cole is going to believe any of this," said Connor, turning to look at Marv, who was rubbing his eyes and shaking his head.

"Do you think?" he mocked. "The best thing to do would be to take you all down to the station…"

"That's not a good idea," said Ven. "I'm afraid the old man and I have somewhere we need to be." He looked at Blake, squashed beneath him. "Wink may have closed the portals by now and they'll all be running around like headless chickens without the big man there, but three Bleachers got through and it would be best to avoid them."

"I need to take a statement from each of you and then get these guys home to their parents," said Marv. "They've been reported as missing."

"Shit, really?" said Olivia.

"I'm going to get it in the neck for this," said Blake.

"Did my mum put posters up yet?" said Mason.

"Erm, no," said Marv.

"It's not too serious then," Mason relaxed.

"Well, you don't need a statement from me or the old man," said Ven. "We're not reported missing and you've no grounds to hold us; we've done nothing wrong."

Marv looked at Ven and then at the old man, who had nodded off and was drooling on to his chin.

"I could hold you on disturbing the peace," said Marv, embarrassed by the idea, but realising he had little else to keep them there.

"Really?" said Ven, astonished and pointing to Vitmyre. "That's disturbing the peace, is it?"

Vitmyre awoke with a start, eyes scanning the inside of the car and settling on Marv.

193

"Marv, is it?" he asked.

"Yeah," Marv replied, warily.

"You've not had much in the way of opportunity of late. Things have gotten a bit stale, haven't they?"

"Erm, yeah…"

"Well, I can see some forks in the road, changes on the horizon… a food receptacle and a mythical creature, travel… opportunity."

"Thanks for the horoscope, but we've got a few more pressing things that we need to sort out," Marv said.

"Like the statue thief at the chapel?" Vitmyre asked.

"Yeah," said Marv, his forehead creased in confusion. "How did you know about that?"

"I know almost everything," he replied.

"Okay, what else do you know?"

"I know the thief is in the chapel now."

Marv and Connor looked at each other.

"How would you know that?" asked Connor.

"I just do," came the simple reply.

"So, if we went in there right now, the thief would be in there and we would catch them?" said Marv.

"Yes."

Marv and Connor looked at each other. It sounded ridiculous, much like listening to one of those clairvoyants off some peripheral television channel and certainly not something that they should or ever would take seriously.

But then, they had just seen the group fall out of a glowing tyre swing. And they had just been chased by tall, very odd and scary-looking men and listened to a story about other universes.

Perhaps that's why they *were* taking it seriously.

"Okay, so here's what's going to happen," Marv began.

"Firstly, we are going to go into the chapel… that's my partner and I and you…" he looked at the old man.

"Anywhere he goes, I go," said Ven.

"Fair enough," Marv agreed. "You three wait in the car until we get back and then we'll drop you off at your parent's houses and you can explain the whole thing to them."

The back row nodded.

Connor grabbed his radio and called in to explain that they had found the three missing persons and were dropping them back at their homes. It felt good to be the ones to have found them, however accidental it had been, and it would no doubt mean some long overdue respect being thrown their way, back at the office. If they could catch the statue thief in the same night, he imagined Cole would just about faint with astonishment. She would certainly need to seriously reconsider a lot of the mean stuff she had ever said about them.

"If we pull all of this off tonight, can you imagine the look on Cole's face?" Connor said, unable to contain the smile spreading across his face.

"I'd give my right leg to see that," said Marv. "Well, not *my* right leg. I'd give your right leg to see it though."

After some awkward shifting of positions in the back of the car, Ven and the old man stepped out and joined Marv and Connor as they walked slowly over to the chapel.

"I'll be honest, I'm not really sure I'll be able to explain any of this to my parents," said Blake, watching the others walk through the chapel gate, from the back seat.

"Nor me," agreed Olivia.

"If *I'm* being honest, this will probably make more sense than most of the things I've ever said to my mum," said Mason.

*

Marv entered the chapel first, pushing the large wooden door carefully, but unable to avoid the creak that accompanied the movement.

The lights were on, warming period wall lights, designed to look like candles, but the chapel was empty and silent, apart from their own footsteps.

"You sure about this?" Marv asked the old man.

"Sure about what?" he replied, momentarily forgetting why he was there.

"About the thief being in here?"

"Oh, that? Yes, quite sure."

Marv scanned the chapel. "Any clue as to where?"

"Not very good at 'detecting' are you, Detective?" Vitmyre said, during a fleeting resurgence of clarity. "Might I suggest a change of career?"

They heard a thump from a room at the far end of the chapel and the group froze. Marv motioned to Connor to head down the aisle and towards the wooden door to the left of the pulpit.

They both crept forward, their eyes on the door as they went. Ven and the old man remained by the pew nearest the main door, away from any potential harm.

As they closed in on the door, they could hear shuffling from within the room, and the dragging of something heavy across the floorboards.

They looked at each other, readying themselves for a confrontation and then Marv quickly turned the handle and opened the door.

*

196

"So, what's your plan?" Olivia asked Blake.

"My plan?"

"After we've told our parents what happened, what are you going to do?"

"I'm not sure," he replied, his vacant expression partially hidden within the dark of the car.

"It's not going to go back to normal, is it?" she sighed. "Even stealing the old man and closing the portals... it's all just a temporary fix. The portals will be back up and running at some point and somebody will just take the old man's place. They'll still come after us, because we took the old man."

"But the old man is the key," said Mason. "At least, I think he is."

"Yeah," Blake agreed. "The old man is the one with the abilities. Without him, they wouldn't know where to look. We'll be safe."

Olivia didn't look so sure.

"I'm starving," said Mason. "We haven't eaten anything all day."

"I've still got half a pack of biscuits in my bedroom," said Blake, smiling at the mere thought of them.

"I think I've got some pasta left," said Mason, clutching at a memory of his cupboards.

"What are you going to have with that?" Blake asked.

"I usually just pour a tin of baked beans over it."

"Beans on pasta?" Blake said, his face scrunched in disapproval.

"You do know they make other food?" Olivia said. "Not just baked beans."

"They're just so versatile."

"Are they?" she asked, keenly disagreeing.

"You can have them with chips, with mashed potato, with pasta, with rice..."

197

"I'm pretty sure you can't have them with rice," she butted in.

"… on toast," he continued, "with cheese, scrambled eggs…"

"Okay, I think we get the idea," she said. "You like baked beans."

"Didn't Jim's old band have a song about beans?" asked Blake.

"Yeah, man," Mason chuckled. "Which band was that?"

"There have been so many," said Olivia, still haunted by her latest experience.

"Piss Rainbow, I think," said Blake.

"I thought that was when they went through their doom grind phase?" Mason tried to recall. "The beans song was more upbeat."

"It might have been His Frequently Chewed Toenails," Blake suggested.

"Could've been," Mason nodded.

"Erm, guys…" Olivia said, alarmed and staring directly into the rear view mirror at the scene of three tall figures in the road, just a few car lengths behind them. "They found us."

FORTY

Marv and Connor stared at the reverend, as he, in turn, stared back at them with surprise.

"Detectives…" he managed, resting the statue on the floor and standing upright to face them.

"Reverend," Marv nodded, looking around the room, perhaps hoping to see signs of an intruder, but noting only old wardrobes and a curtained area at the back of the dusty room.

"Just er… just having a bit of a tidy round," the reverend said. "Would you like a cup of tea? I was just about to have one."

"No, thanks," he replied, walking slowly into the room now and having a closer look at the statue, that the reverend had been moving.

Marv didn't say anything, but wandered over to the curtain and drew it back to find several statues stood in the corner.

"I think you might owe us an explanation," said Connor, as both detectives stared at the man.

He didn't respond straight away, no doubt weighing up his options for a few seconds.

"I understand how this looks," he eventually replied.

"Really?" Marv asked. "Because it sort of looks like you have all the missing statues in here, but that can't be right, can it? I mean, why would you steal your own statues?"

"I haven't stolen them," he protested. "Just moving them, that's all."

"And why would you do that?"

The reverend's shoulders dropped, fully appreciating the situation.

"Please, don't judge me," he said, slumping into a threadbare chair behind him. "I'm really not stealing the statues… I fully intend to put them all back."

They looked hard at him, silent, waiting for an explanation.

"I'm under a lot of pressure at the minute," he began. "The bishop of my diocese is coming down hard on dwindling congregations and well, the short and tall of it is that I have to get the numbers up, if the chapel is to survive. If I don't, they'll end up selling the building off to developers; I've seen it happen to colleagues of mine and I'm too old to be uprooted and thrown into the mix in some big city church. Arseholes to that. I like it here, detectives."

"And so you stole your own statues?" asked Connor.

"I actually broke the first one, it was an accident. One of the parishioners asked where it had gone and… well, I just told him it had disappeared. I don't know why I lied, it just came out. He said that was odd and that maybe something spooky was going on. That's when I got the idea to take the others and hide them. Word soon got around that something strange was going on and sure enough, we got a lot more visitors to the chapel; ghost hunters and the like; a new generation of potential followers and even if only a handful of them stick around, it's something. The others at least donate money for the privilege of an hour or two searching for spirits."

"Look," said Marv. "I don't know where the law stands on pretending there's a ghost in your church, but I can tell you that there is definitely a law against wasting police time."

"I'm so sorry, detective. I didn't mean for it to go this far."

"Do you know how many hours we've sat outside in the car, drinking shit coffee, trying to stay awake through the night, hoping to catch the thief?" Marv vented.

"I know and again, I'm so very sorry."

"It was *really* shit coffee," Marv stressed.

"I started out with the best of intentions."

"Let's go," Marv said to his colleague, before turning and heading out of the room and into the chapel. "We'll be in touch," he added, as Connor set off behind him.

They walked back down the aisle, looking at Ven and the old man, staring out through the main doorway to the street beyond.

"We have a situation here," said Ven, looking at the Bleachers walking down the road towards the car.

*

"Are the keys in the ignition?" asked Olivia.

Blake leaned forward, his head peering above the headrest to the driver's seat.

"No," he replied.

"Shit!" she shouted. "Now what?"

"Let's make a run for it!" said Mason, already opening the car door and clambering clumsily out on to the tarmac.

"How did they even find us?" cursed Blake, as he too hurried awkwardly from the vehicle, Olivia hopping out of the same side after him.

They started to run in the opposite direction to the Bleachers, along the road, towards the park. Mason turned to see that the Bleachers had picked up their pace and were sprinting after them, but not before one had pulled the tracking device from the car bumper.

He cursed inwardly, not wanting to part with any breath unnecessarily, but needing to share his theory.

"It wasn't a stone they threw at the back of the car..." he said between heavy breaths. "...some sort of tracking device...I think."

"What?" Blake called to him, without looking back.

"Some sort of... tracking device..."

"Trapping the mice?" Blake struggled to hear his friend over the sound of his own feet on the tarmac and the rush of blood, thumping through his head.

"Mice?"

"I can't hear you!"

"I said 'device', a tracking... it doesn't matter," Mason concluded, unable to combine talking and running.

The black metal gate to the park was still open – it was often closed as soon as it went dark, but clearly the park attendant was running late or shirking his duties. The group ran through, eyes focused firmly on the way ahead and on the tarmac path winding through the small park. It was dark and the only light came from a couple of street lights running the length of the park's railings. This meant that it only got darker, the deeper they ran into the park, though a right turn up ahead would soon see them exit the park, via another metal gate. Hopefully that too would be still open.

FORTY ONE

Arthur awoke with a start and was startled to find a white cat licking his face. He pushed it from his lap and took a moment to gather his senses.

He had fallen asleep in his deck chair again; third time this week. Luckily, it hadn't rained and the heavy cloud cover had meant the temperature hadn't dropped too much once the sun had disappeared, but he would have to start making a concerted effort to stay awake. A month or two down the line and the evenings would be much cooler. He didn't want to catch pneumonia.

The light flickered from the cluttered shed behind him, somehow illustrating his fragmented waking process. The cat looked on, sat patiently, head tilted to one side.

For a time the two simply looked at each other, two beings locked in a moment and then the cat turned its attention to the park that ran behind the allotments.

Arthur heard the distant voices, but couldn't make sense of them. Was it young kids making a nuisance of themselves? Chapel-on-the-Moss didn't have a particular problem with wayward youth, but he had seen enough programmes and news articles to be ready for such an eventuality.

He stood and hobbled into his shed, rummaging amongst the clutter until he found his trusty old spade. He grabbed it and emerged from the shed like a knight would emerge with a long sword, emboldened and ready for trouble.

*

Blake reached the gate first, thanking the powers that be that it was still open. They were still running, although their pace had slowed and their lungs were struggling with the demands being placed on them.

They paused at the gate, only then looking back through the park as they gulped down the air.

"I'm not... used to... running..." Olivia managed.

"I need... to stop... smoking," Mason coughed.

Blake could see the Bleachers in pursuit, their dark, lumbering shapes hoofing towards them.

"We need to go," he said, before turning through the gate and on down the path between the woods on their left and the allotments on their right.

205

As they went, Blake noticed the light on in Arthur's shed, but couldn't see the man himself. Perhaps he had gone home and forgotten to turn it off. He wouldn't still be out at this time.

They continued to run, veering left on to the woodland track that would eventually snake its way to the river. It was a path that Blake and Olivia knew well, one that they had used since childhood and one that they thought might give them an advantage.

The Bleachers reached the park gate, their own pace slowing, due to their hefty stature, but their determination remained the same. They saw the group turn off into the woods and they continued after them, eyes always on their quarry.

They were running in single file now, along the narrow path, with the allotments to their right, the first and second of them heading towards the woodland path and the last of them flagging a little behind the others.

That was the Bleacher that took the full force of the spade to his face. His legs went from under him and he slammed hard on to his back. If the other Bleachers heard the clang, they took no notice of it, indomitable as they were, relentless in their pursuit of the group.

Arthur looked down at the unconscious Bleacher.

"Not smiling now, are you?" he said to himself, before returning to his shed again and emerging with some plastic cable ties. By this point, he could hear another group of people appearing from out of the park. He could vaguely make out the detectives in the dark and they spotted him too, as they approached.

Marv looked down at the tall, bald-headed cretin, lying still on the ground and snoring fitfully through a mouth full of spittle.

He nodded to Arthur, mainly due to the fact that he didn't have the breath spare to use on words.

"Clumsy bastard ran into my spade, detective," Arthur said. "I don't reckon he'll be too impressed when he comes round." He handed Connor the cables ties over the allotment fence.

"Thanks," said Connor. He rolled the body over and started to apply the ties to the Bleacher's wrists, pinning them behind his back.

Arthur spotted Ven and an old man, catching up to them.

"This why you wanted the chip out, is it?" he asked.

"Yeah," said Ven.

"Two more headed into the woods," he said. "They were after my friends, detectives," he added. "They're good kids."

"I know," Marv replied. "We're on it."

With that, the detectives hurried off into the woods, leaving Ven and the old man looking down at the Bleacher.

"I reared these from a young age," said the old man. "Taught them the ropes…"

"Brainwashed them, you mean," said Ven.

"Gave them a purpose, is all," he replied, somewhat lost in thought. "All part of the big plan."

"And what plan was that?" Arthur asked.

"To beat Fate at her own game," the old man said, softly, as if the realisation brought only regret.

"I'll stay and keep an eye on the Bleacher," said Ven, wanting to reassure Arthur.

"I'd rather you helped my friends, if you can," he replied. "I can keep an eye on this thing."

"Okay," Ven agreed. He took the arm of the old man. "Let's go."

"You're a good man, Arthur," said Vitmyre, as they went. "Next year's beetroot will be the stuff of legend."

*

Blake took large strides through the undergrowth, off the path now and through the trees.

"Where are we going, man?" asked Mason, inwardly cursing at the thorns scratching at his legs.

"There's an old stone hide by the river," said Blake

"I remember that," said Olivia. "We used to play down there as kids."

They waded through thick brush before reaching the banking to the river and sure enough, they could make out the small stone hide nestled into the bank, dark though it was.

"Let's get inside," said Blake, urging the others to follow quickly behind him.

They entered the hide by the side facing the river, through an open doorway. It smelled of damp soil in there, not entirely unexpected given its location.

They crouched, the ceiling too low to accommodate anyone over five feet. It had seemed so big to them as kids and they had still been just that the last time they had frequented the place. They could hear the steady trickle of the river, the water dancing across rocks and lapping against stone outcrops.

And then another noise, further away and behind them... twigs breaking.

"Shit," whispered Blake. Had they picked up their trail so soon?

"We can't stay in here," said Olivia, quietly. "We'll be trapped if they find us."

Blake agreed. "Okay," he replied and moved towards the doorway, looking out at the speckles of occasional moonlight hitting the water, as it filtered through the trees and down to the river.

He took a deep breath and then led them out on to the riverbank. A little further up the banking, the Bleachers stood waiting, their awkward smiles somehow managing to unnaturally penetrate the dark.

Their hearts sank.

"Man, I can't believe I just ran all that way and still got caught," said Mason. "What a waste."

"It is pointless trying to run," called one of the two Bleachers. "We will only find you."

Blake looked around at the woods and then the river, contemplating routes of escape, though he knew there was no route over the river this far into the woods.

"Do you even know why you're still chasing us?" asked Olivia, frustrated and tired of running. "Zenith is over. It's finished. We have the old man."

The Bleachers looked quizzically at each other.

"It's true," confirmed Blake.

"Vitmyre's end was inevitable," said the Bleacher on the left. "Change too is inevitable. There are policies in place for such an eventuality."

"I don't imagine they amount to much," said Olivia. "You don't provide much of a service without the all-knowing 'star of the show'."

"On the contrary. Much of our operation relies on technology these days," said the Bleacher on the right. "The old man, in truth, has been relatively unreliable for a number of years."

"Technology can't replicate the old man's abilities," said Mason.

209

"Algorithms," said the Bleacher.

Mason shook his head. "That's just guessing," he replied. "That doesn't rival 'knowing'. There's too much room for error. You'll make wrong decisions, based on wrong information and the company will fail."

"Then we will simply take the old man back," said the Bleacher, looking over the group and into the woods behind them, as the two detectives stumbled into view, followed closely by Ven and the old man.

"Blake?" Ven called.

"Just down here," he called back.

Ven watched as the Bleachers both removed a device from inside their coats. They were narrow and twice the length of a pen, the end sections of which were shining a menacing yellow.

"Just wait there," Ven shouted, recognising, even from a distance, what those new devices were. "It's too late for all that. You've lost!"

"These are Erasing Charges," said the Bleacher on the left.

"I know what they are," said Ven.

"We could take out two of you on each charge. So, I think we'll be taking the old man back with us." The Bleacher smiled, sickly sweet and smug too.

"Tenacious things, aren't they?" chuckled Vitmyre. "It's instilled into them, of course. Can't quite recall what I called them... beach bums or something... remarkable really." His voice had an elitist ring to it, though now with an element of uncertainty, brought forth with age and senility.

"Things have to change," said Ven. "They can't go back to the way they were." He was addressing the Bleachers, but he hoped some of what he was saying would resonate on some level with the old man too.

210

"Change is inevitable," repeated the Bleacher.

"Change for the better," Ven added.

"Give us the old man."

Ven looked at the detectives, but they were entirely out of their depth. Both looked like they wanted to say something, to step in and treat the whole affair as a routine situation, but they knew full well that it was anything but routine.

The old man looked bewildered in one moment and then staunch in the next, as if a younger version of himself was relishing the stand-off, proud of his proselytised subordinates, but then the older self would take over, tainted with regret and confusion.

Ven noticed the white cat first. It walked by him and down towards the river. It stood in front of Blake and Olivia, looking out at the Bleachers. Mason spotted it shortly after Blake, as it sat on the ground in front of them.

Then they all began to notice the white doves in the trees, a handful at first, quite difficult to spot in the dark, but the branches were soon filled with them, still, eerie in their silence, all watching the Bleachers.

It wasn't lost on the Bleachers either, their smiles beginning to slip as the strangeness of the situation started to unfold.

Olivia noticed a handful of white mice scurry by her feet in the direction of the cat. They lined up next to it.

Within a minute, the whole woodland seemed to be flooded with white. Owls, moths, spiders... the dark woodland seemed to glow strangely with what looked like a moving snow of creatures.

"I did wonder if I would ever get to see her again," said Vitmyre, smiling wistfully, though his eyes relayed his fear.

And then they all felt her presence, there in the woods with them. It was like being washed with a warm purity.

211

She clung to the shadows, tall, her hair a black tangle of shadow and branches, as if one with the trees.

She reached the Bleachers first, sometimes only her eyes visible in the dark, but occasionally her form fell solid under the moonlight. She looked each of the Bleachers deep in their eyes, searching for something within them.

"No," she whispered, before leaving them and returning to the shadows of the trees.

The ends of their devices started to glow a bright yellow as they tried desperately to let go of them, but their hands were no longer their own. Though they struggled against the inescapable, they were struck by the shadows, each blow erasing a part of them; an arm, an eye, a leg, until there was nothing left of them.

Everybody looked around, at each other and at the woodland, still washed in the ghostly bluish-white of creatures penetrating the darkness.

And then the shadow woman was between the old man and Ven.

She glanced down at Ven first, some warmth behind her eyes as she revealed a little more of her full form, still draped in shadows, as if in robes, but her face clear.

It was still difficult too for the others to see her properly in the dark, but she was wraithlike and beautiful all at once. Ven was entranced by her immediately.

So this was Fate. Had he been right to put his faith in her?

She looked down at the old man now, who stared nervously back.

"Long have I waited for this day," she began, calmly. "How safe you have been, in your own private universe and it has been no easy feat bringing you into this one." She looked him over with hard eyes. "Time has not been kind to you."

"And yet, you look the same as the day I left," he replied, flattering her without particularly meaning to; she was exactly as he remembered her.

"I'm not sure you understand the gravity of the situation," she said, holding her gaze firmly.

"What I did, I did to prove a point…"

"What you did was against all ancient laws. Only Gods can…"

"Why?" he interrupted her. "Why is it that only Gods should have all the fun?"

"Has your forbidden enterprise taught you nothing?" she asked. "Has any of that knowledge been fun?"

"Well…"

"No," she answered for him. "The very weight of it has broken your mind; you are a shell of your former self. You were full of potential back then; that is the sadness of it. You could have done great things…"

"I did do great things!" he argued.

"Zenith? You think Zenith was great?"

"Its very existence is great. It shows that you don't have to be a God to control destiny."

"All you've shown is that it should *only* be a God that controls destiny! You used whatever power you had for personal gain, for resources. A God would never do that," she accused him. "I do what I do to keep an order to the universe, to keep it from tearing itself apart. Every last detail is considered and weighed against the greater good. Many of your decisions have been made based entirely on how you stood to profit as a company. Destiny cannot be privatised."

"And so you think this power belongs only to the Gods?" he asked.

213

"It has forever been so," she replied. "It is the way of things. Our universe came first. The emergence and development of this universe is in large part down to the insistence of Gods. It is what we do."

"But that doesn't mean we can't do it too," said the old man.

"You stole from me."

He lowered his head, accepting of his ill deed, exhausted.

"I did," he acknowledged. "Ambition was a demon within me and sadly one that I couldn't shake. And in truth, the weight of knowledge has taken its toll; time hasn't been kind. I have grown tired."

He looked up at her again, all fight having left him, actually glad to have been caught.

"You will return with me," she decreed.

"I understand."

She turned her attention to Ven, stood next to the old man.

"Thank you, Ven," she said, with something of a smile. "Your faith and conviction have been paramount in this endeavour."

"Thank you," he said, wondering if he should bow.

She smiled fully now, seeing something behind his eyes. "I see your future disappears very soon," she revealed. "I get the feeling you know what that means."

"I have somewhere else to be," he yielded.

"Happy trails, then," she said. "Don't be a stranger."

And then she was facing the group; Blake, Olivia and Mason staring back at her with awe from the bottom of the banking.

She regarded them one at a time, left to right.

"Thank you all," she said.

"Can I ask you something?" said Mason.

She looked his way and raised her eyebrows in anticipation of the question.

"Do fae folk exist?"

She smiled again. "Do you want them to?"

"Erm… yeah."

"Then they do."

Mason wasn't entirely sure if that meant they did or not, but bowed his head in thanks anyway.

"You all have wonderful journeys ahead of you," she said, before turning to the detectives.

Marv took a startled step back and gulped down his fright at seeing the shadowed woman up close.

"You've been wanting a change," she said.

"I have," he nervously replied.

"Not long to wait," she assured him.

"I have a mortgage, I can't just leave my job…" he began.

"Have faith. You'll manage."

And then she looked at Connor.

"Do I get a promotion?" he asked, tentatively.

"Do you want one?" she asked.

"Erm… yeah."

"Then you will."

And then she was simply gone, vanished into the darkness, leaving them all wondering if she had actually been there at all.

Ven looked to his side and realised that the old man was gone too.

Collectively they all seemed to let out a huge breath, as if they hadn't breathed for the last ten minutes.

"That just happened, didn't it?" said Blake.

"I think so," said Olivia.

The doves began to take flight from the trees and the bluish snow of creatures gradually fell away into darkness once again. Only the cat remained for a moment, looking around the group, before it too patted off through the trees.

215

"Anyone else need a drink?" asked Connor.

"Yes," agreed everybody.

"I know just the place," said Olivia.

EPILOGUE

It was a typical student bar; guitars stuck to the ceiling, posters of bands covering every inch of the walls, faux-Victorian lighting. Marv remembered the likes from his youth, in the days when he used to string together a few chords and shout broadly political noise down the microphone. It was a world away from where he ended up, of course, but then he had never really expected to 'make it'. He supposed, in hindsight, it had just been his way of trying to be relevant as a teenager and it had certainly been fun.

At just five weeks, it had been possibly one of the shortest band 'careers' in history, but looking around the place and noting the equipment set up on the stage made him almost wish he was still back there. He put it down to nostalgia; that and the fact that they were all still high from their meeting with Fate.

"Cheers," said Ven, holding up his pint of beer.

They all raised their drinks. "Cheers."

The round table to the right of the stage seated all six of them, comfortably.

"Do you think Arthur will be okay?" asked Olivia, concerned for the old man at the allotment.

"He needed a swig of his hip flask after seeing Fate show up and 'disappear' the Bleacher, but he seemed okay," replied Blake, taking a drink. "He said he was going for an early night, then mentioned something about beetroot... I tuned out a bit at that point."

"I can't believe we actually met Fate," Olivia smiled.

"I can't believe any of it," said Blake. "It's all a bit mad."

"Imagine knowing everything," said Mason, still awed by the presence of the God in the woods.

"I don't think I'd like it," said Blake. "I kind of like not knowing stuff."

"You're very good at it," laughed Olivia.

"Ha ha," Blake smiled. "So, what's next, Ven?"

"I'm going to check out this 'other place', see what it's like."

"Let me know if it's any good, man," said Mason. "I'll come and visit."

"I will," said Ven. "It will be good to catch up."

"What about you, detectives?"

"Well, we'll probably have this pint and then get some sleep," said Marv.

"Yeah, after solving two cases in one night, the troll gave us a few days off," Connor added.

"You staying for the band?" asked Olivia. "They're mostly awful, but..." she struggled to finish the sentence, "...but they're also quite loud."

218

"I actually used to be in a band, back in the day," Marv said.

"Really?" asked Connor, almost spitting his beer out in surprise.

"Yeah, little bit punk, not very good."

"Wow. I did not know that."

"I rarely mention it. It was a long time ago. Our old drummer still has a recording studio out in the old factory buildings in town."

And then the band wandered out on to the stage; the drummer first, wearing a bowler hat; the bass player, insanely tall and wearing clothes far too small for him; a guitarist with the dirtiest looking jeans Marv had ever seen and a singer sporting the most hideous mustard coloured cardigan.

"We're Melted Clown Lunchbox and what you are about to hear is your own fault," said the singer.

"That's Jim," said Olivia. "He's not really a 'people person'."

And then the music kicked in, a blistering stage full of sonic violence and it made Marv smile. He instantly felt like a teenager again, his mind transported back to his youth and his own social disconnect.

It was a short number, ending abruptly, followed by a few moments of relative quiet, as the singer poured himself some tea from a flask and the bass player hit the occasional note for effect.

"This is great," said Marv, leaning over the table to Blake.

"It's definitely different," he sort of agreed.

"Have they recorded anything?" he asked.

"Not that I know of," Blake replied. "Why, you going to hook them up?"

He thought for a moment. "I suppose I could," he finally said. "I think Jim would appreciate that, they could use a manager."

Marv smiled, as somewhere across the universe his destiny fell into place.

219

THE END

Why do things work out the way they do?

by Melted Clown Lunchbox

Things, all things
I find absurd
When you cook, it's nice
When I cook, it's turd
You get the most purple Skittles
My bag has the least
When you iron, it's neat
When I iron, it's still creased

Oy you, why do things work out the way they do?

Stuff, all stuff
Gets on my tits
Your curry is nice
Mine gives me the shits
Your boss is caring
Mine's a son of a bitch
Your shampoo works
Mine makes me itch

Oy you, why do things work out the way they do?

Oy.

More comedy from Carl Lee;

THE TROUSER TRILOGY

Life took a very weird turn for Emery Trouser, when a portal to Hell opened in his kitchen.

From that moment onwards he would become embroiled in a series of dizzying adventures that would see him pitted against malign forces from other worlds, partnered with numerous characters, both alive and otherwise.

TROUSER'S EDGE
ONCE UPON A HELL
EMERY AT THE GATES

AVAILABLE NOW FROM DURGE PULP

Printed in Great Britain
by Amazon